THE RAGMAN'S DAUGHTER

'Alan Sillitoe stands as a comforting reminder to the English that the grand old roistering "low life" tradition of Fielding and Dickens is not yet dead, and a welcome antidote to writers like John Osborne, Kingsley Amis and John Braine, who have used working-class values and aspirations to bludgeon middle-class hypocrisies, and whose characters are always trying to move in social circles for which their family backgrounds clearly unfit them ... There can be no doubt that working-class life has a reality, a special kind of *presence*, in England which it has not had in America for a very long time ... *The Ragman's Daughter* has been made into a successful film, directed by Harold Becker.'—New York Herald Tribune

'Shows him at his best, better even than in *Saturday Night and Sunday Morning*.'—Books and Bookmen

Also by Alan Sillitoe

Fiction
SATURDAY NIGHT AND SUNDAY MORNING
THE LONELINESS OF THE LONG-DISTANCE RUNNER
THE GENERAL
KEY TO THE DOOR
THE DEATH OF WILLIAM POSTERS
A TREE ON FIRE
GUZMAN, GO HOME
A START IN LIFE
TRAVELS IN NIHILON
RAW MATERIAL
MEN WOMEN AND CHILDREN
THE FLAME OF LIFE

Non-Fiction
MOUNTAINS AND CAVERNS

Poetry
THE RATS AND OTHER POEMS
A FALLING OUT OF LOVE AND OTHER POEMS
LOVE IN THE ENVIRONS OF VORONEZH
STORM AND OTHER POEMS

Travel
ROAD TO VOLGOGRAD

Play
ALL CITIZENS ARE SOLDIERS
(with Ruth Fainlight)

THE RAGMAN'S DAUGHTER

Alan Sillitoe

W. H. ALLEN · LONDON
A Howard & Wyndham Company

Printed in Great Britain by
Fletcher & Son Ltd, Norwich
for the Publishers, W. H. Allen & Co. Ltd,
44 Hill Street, London W1X 8LB

Bound by Richard Clay (The Chaucer Press) Ltd,
Bungay, Suffolk

ISBN 0 491 01728 6

ACKNOWLEDGEMENTS

The Guardian; Pick of Today's Short Stories; Argosy; New Statesman; Transatlantic Review; The Daily Worker; London Magazine; New Yorker.

CONTENTS

THE RAGMAN'S DAUGHTER

I was walking home with an empty suitcase one night, an up-to-date pigskin zip job I was fetching back from a pal who thought he'd borrowed it for good, and two plain-clothed coppers stopped me. They questioned me for twenty minutes, then gave up and let me go. While they had been talking to me, a smash-and-grab had taken place around the corner, and ten thousand nicker had vanished into the wide open spaces of somebody who needed it.

That's life. I was lucky my suitcase had nothing but air in it. Sometimes I walk out with a box of butter and cheese from the warehouse I work at, but for once that no-good God was on my side—trying to make up for the times he's stabbed me in the back maybe. But if the coppers had had a word with me a few nights later they'd have found me loaded with high-class provision snap.

My job is unloading cheeses as big as beer barrels off lorries that come in twice a week from the country. They draw in at the side door of the warehouse, and me and a couple of mates roll our sleeves up and shoulder them slowly down the gang-plank into the special part set aside for cheeses. We once saw, after checking the lists, that there was one cheese extra, so decided to share it out between a dozen of us and take it home to our wives and families. The question came up as to which cheese we should get rid of, and the chargehand said: 'Now, all look around for the cheese that the rats have started to go for, and that's the one we'll carve between us, because you can bet your bottom dollar that that's the best.'

It was a load of choice Dalbeattie, and I'd never tasted any cheese so delicious. For a long time my wife would say: 'When are you going to get us some more of that marvellous cheese, Tony?' And whatever I did take after that never seemed to satisfy them, though every time I went out with a chunk of

9

cheese or a fist of butter I was risking my job, such as it is. Once for a treat I actually bought a piece of Dalbeattie from another shop, but they knew it wasn't stolen so it didn't taste as good as the other that the rats had pointed out to us. It happens now and again at the warehouse that a bloke takes some butter and the police nab him. They bring him back and he gets the push. Fancy getting the push for half a pound of butter. I'd be ashamed to look my mates in the eye again, and would be glad I'd got the sack so's I wouldn't have to.

The first thing I stole was at infants school when I was five. They gave us cardboard coins to play with, pennies, shillings, half-crowns, stiff and almost hard to bend, that we were supposed to exchange for bricks and pieces of chalk. This lesson was called Buying and Selling. Even at the time I remember feeling that there was something not right about the game, yet only pouting and playing it badly because I wasn't old enough to realize what it was. But when I played well I ended up the loser, until I learned quickly that one can go beyond skill: at the end of the next afternoon I kept about a dozen of the coins (silver I noticed later) in my pocket when the teacher came round to collect them back.

'Some is missing,' she said, in that plummy voice that sent shivers down my spine and made me want to give them up. But I resisted my natural inclinations and held out. 'Someone hasn't given their money back,' she said. 'Come along, children, own up, or I'll keep you in after all the other classes have gone home.'

I was hoping she'd search me, but she kept us in for ten minutes, and I went home with my pockets full. That night I was caught by a shopkeeper trying to force the coins into his fag and chewing-gum machines. He dragged me home and the old man lammed into me. So, sobbing up to bed, I learned at an early age that money meant trouble as well.

Next time at school I helped myself to bricks, but teacher saw my bulging pockets and took them back, then threw me into the playground, saying I wasn't fit to be at school. This showed me that it was always safest to go for money.

Once, an uncle asked what I wanted to be when I grew up,

and I answered: 'A thief'. He bumped me, so I decided, whenever anybody else asked that trick question to say: 'An honest man' or 'An engine driver'. I stole money from my mother's purse, or odd coppers left lying around the house for gas or electricity, and so I got batted for that as well as for saying I wanted to be a thief when I grew up. I began to see that really I was getting clobbered for the same thing, which made me keep my trap shut on the one hand, and not get caught on the other.

In spite of the fact that I nicked whatever I could lay my hands on without too much chance of getting caught, I didn't like possessing things. Suits, a car, watches—as soon as I nicked something and got clear away, I lost interest in it. I broke into an office and came out with two typewriters, and after having them at home for a day I borrowed a car and dropped them over Trent bridge one dark night. If the cops cared to dredge the river about there they'd get a few surprises. What I like most is the splash stuff makes when I drop it in: that plunge into water of something heavy—such as a TV set, a cash register and once, best of all, a motorbike—which makes a dull exploding noise and has the same effect on me as booze (which I hate) because it makes my head spin. Even a week later, riding on a bus, I'll suddenly twitch and burst out laughing at the thought of it, and some posh trot will tut-tut, saying: 'These young men! Drunk at eleven in the morning! What they want is to be in the army.'

If I lost all I have in the world I wouldn't worry much. If I was to go across the road for a packet of fags one morning and come back to see the house clapping its hands in flames with everything I owned burning inside I'd turn my back without any thought or regret and walk away, even if my jacket and last ten-bob note were in the flames as well.

What I'd like, believe it or not, is to live in a country where I didn't like thieving and where I didn't want to thieve, a place where everybody felt the same way because they all had only the same as everyone else—even if it wasn't much. Jail is a place like this, though it's not the one I'd find agreeable because you aren't free there. The place that fills my mind would be the same as in jail because everybody would have the same, but being free as well they wouldn't want to nick what bit each had got. I don't know what sort of system that would be called.

While as a youth I went out with girls, I used to like thieving more. The best of all was when I got a young girl to come thieving with me. The right sort was better than any mate I could team up with, more exciting and safe.

I met Doris outside a fish-and-chip shop on Ilkeston Road. Going in to get a supply for supper she dropped her purse, and a few obstinate shekels rolled into the road. 'Don't worry,' I said, 'I'll find them, duck.'

A couple of other youths wanted to help, but I got one by the elbow. 'Bale out. She's my girl-friend. You'll get crippled for life.'

'All right, Tony,' he laughed. 'I didn't know it was you.'

I picked her money up: 'This is the lot'—followed her into the light of the fish-and-chip shop where I could see what she was made of. 'I'm going for some chips as well,' I said, so as not to put her off.

'Thanks for getting my money. I have butterfingers sometimes.' Her hair was the colour of butter, yellow and reaching for her shoulders, where my hands wanted to be. We stood in the queue. I'd just eaten a bundle of fish-and-chips downtown, so even the smell in this joint turned my guts. 'Haven't I seen you somewhere before?' I asked.

'You might, for all I know. I've been around nearly as long as you have.'

'Where do you live, then?'

'Up Churchfield Lane.'

'I'll see you home.'

'You won't.' She was so fair and goodlooking that I almost lost heart, though not enough to stop me answering: 'You might drop your purse again.' I didn't know whether I'd passed her on the street some time, dreamed about her, or seen her drifting across the television screen in a shampoo advertisement between "Blood Gun" and "The Kremlin Strikes Again". Her skin was smooth, cheeks a bit meaty, eyes blue, small nose and lips also fleshy but wearing a camouflage of orange-coloured lipstick that made me want to kiss them even more than if it had been flag-red. She stood at the counter with a vacant, faraway look in her eyes, the sort that meant she had a bit more thought in her rather than the other way round. She gave a little sniff at the billowing clouds of chip steam doubled in size because of mirrors behind the sizzling bins. It was impossible to tell whether or not she liked the smell.

'You're a long way from Churchfield Lane,' I said. 'Ain't you got chip shops up that part?'

'Dad says they do good fish here,' she told me. 'So I come to get him some, as a favour.'

'It's better at Rawson's though, downtown. You ought to let me take you there some time—for a supper. You'd enjoy it.'

It was her turn at the counter. 'I'm busy these days. Two shillings worth of chips and six fish, please.'

'Where do you work, then?'

'I don't.'

I laughed: 'Neither do I.'

She took her bundle: 'Thank you very much'—turned to me: 'You won't be able to take me out then, will you?'

I edged a way back to the door, and we stood on the pavement. 'You're a torment, as well as being goodlooking. I've still got money, even if I don't go to work right now.' We walked across the road, and all the time I was waiting for her to tell me to skid, hoping she would yet not wanting her to. 'Does it fall from heaven, then?'

'No, I nick it.'

She half believed me. 'I'll bet you do. Where from?'

'It all depends. Anywhere.' I could already see myself taking her the whole way home—if I kept my trap flapping.

'I've never stolen anything in my life,' she said, 'but I've often wanted to.'

'If you stick around I'll show you a few things.'

She laughed: 'I might be scared.'

'Not with me. We'll go out one night and see what we can do.'

'Fast worker. We could do it for kicks, though.'

'It's better to do it for money,' I said, dead strict on this.

'What's the difference? It's stealing.'

I'd never thought about it this way before. 'Maybe it is. But it's still not the same.'

'If you do it for kicks,' she went on, 'you don't get caught so easily.'

'There's no point in doing something just for kicks,' I argued. 'It's a waste of time.'

'Well,' she said, 'I'll tell you what. You do it for money, and I'll do it for kicks. Then we'll both be satisfied.'

'Fine,' I said, taking her arm, 'that sounds reasonable.'

She lived in a big old house just off Churchfield Lane, and I even got a kiss out of her before she went into the garden and called me a soft good night. Doris, she had said, my name's Doris.

I thought she was joking about stealing stuff for kicks, but I met her a few days later outside a cinema, and when the show was over and we stood by a pavement where five roads met, she said: 'I suppose you just prowl around until you see something that's easy and quiet.'

'More or less'—not showing my surprise. 'It might be a bit harder than that though.' I held up a jack knife, that looked like a hedgehog with every blade splayed out: 'That one ain't for opening pop bottles; and this one ain't for getting stones out of horses hoofs either. A useful little machine, this is.'

'I thought you used hairgrips?' She was treating it like a joke, but I said, deadpan: 'Sometimes. Depends on the lock.' A copper walked across the road towards us, and with every flat footstep I closed a blade of the knife, slipping it into my pocket before he was half-way over. 'Come on,' I said, lighting a fag, and heading towards Berridge Road.

The overhead lights made us look TB, as if some big government scab had made a mistake on the telephone and had too much milk tipped into the sea. We even stopped talking at the sight of each other's fag-ash faces, but after a while the darker side streets brought us back to life, and every ten yards I got what she'd not been ready to give on the back seat of the pictures: a fully-fledged passionate kiss. Into each went all my wondering at why a girl like this should want to come out on nightwork with a lout called me.

'You live in a big house,' I said when we walked on. 'What does your old man do?'

'He's a scrapdealer.'

'Scrapdealer?' It seemed funny, somehow. 'No kidding?'

'You know—rag and metal merchant. Randall's on Orston Road.'

I laughed, because during my life as a kid that was the place I'd taken scrap-iron and jamjars, lead and woollens to, and her old man was the bloke who'd traded with me—a deadbeat skinflint with a pound note sign between his eyes and breathing LSD all over the place. Dead at the brain and crotch the fat gett drove a maroon Jaguar in an old lounge suit. I'd seen him one day scatter a load of kids in the street, pumping that screaming button-hooter before he got too close, and as they bulletted out of his way throw a fistful of change after them. He nearly smashed into a lamp-post because such sudden and treacherous generosity put him off his steering.

'What's funny about it?' she wanted to know.

'I'm surprised, that's all.'

'I told a girl at school once that my dad was a scrapdealer, and she laughed, just like you did. I don't see what's funny about it at all.' You stupid bastard, I called myself, laughing for nothing when before you'd been getting marvellous kisses from her. A black cat shot through the light of a lamp-post, taking my good luck with it.

'He's better off tl an most people, so maybe you laugh because you're jealous.'

'Not me,' I said, trying to make amends. 'Another reason I laughed, if you want to know the truth, is that I've always wanted to be a scrapdealer, but so far I've never known how to get started. It was just the coincidence.' While she was wondering whether to believe me I tried changing the subject: 'What sort of a school did you go to where they'd laugh at a thing like that?'

'I still go,' she said, 'a grammar school. I leave at the end of

the year, though.' A school kid, I thought. Still, she's a posh
one, so she can be nearly seventeen, though she looks at least
as old as me, which is eighteen and a half. 'I'll be glad to leave
school, anyway. I want to be independent. I'm always in top
class though, so in a sense I like it as well. Funny.'

'You want to get a job, you mean?'

'Sure. Of course. I'll go to a secretarial college. Dad says
he'd let me.'

'Sounds all right. You'll be set for life, the way you're
going.' We were walking miles, pacing innumerable streets
out of our systems, a slow arm-in-arm zig-zag through the
darkening neighbourhood. It was a night full of star holes
after a day of rain, a windy sky stretching into a huge flow
over the rising ground of Forest Fields and Hyson Green
and Basford, through Mapperly to Redhill and carried away
by some red doubledecker loaded with colliers vanishing into
the black night of Sherwood. We made a solitary boat in this
flood of small houses, packed together like the frozen teeth
of sharp black waves and, going from one lighthouse lamp-
post to another, the district seemed an even bigger stretch
than the area I was born and brought up in.

An old woman stood on a doorstep saying: 'Have you got a
fag, my duck? I'd be ever so grateful if you could manage it.'
She looked about ninety, and when I handed her one she lit
up as if ready to have a nervous breakdown. 'Thanks, my love.
I hope you'll be happy, the pair of you.'

'Same to you, missis,' I said as we went off.

'Aren't old women funny?' Doris said.

We kissed at every corner, and whenever it seemed I might
not she reminded me by a tug at my linked arm. She wore
slacks and a head scarf, a three-quarter leather coat and flat-
heeled lace-ups, as if this was her idea of a break-and-entry rig.
She looked good in it, stayed serious and quiet for most of the
walking, so that all we did now and again was move into a
clinch for a good bout of tormenting kisses. She moaned
softly sometimes, and I wanted to go further than lipwork, but
how could we in a solid wide open street where someone
walking through would disturb us? With the air so sweet and

long lasting, I knew it would be a stretch past her bed time
before she finally landed home that night. Yet I didn't care,
felt awake and marvellous, full of love for all the world—
meaning her first and then myself, and it showed in our kisses
as we went at a slow rate through the streets, arms fast around
each other like Siamese twins.

Across the main road stretched a wall covering the yard
of a small car-body workshop. As soon as I saw it my left leg
began trembling and the kneecap of my right to twitch, so I
knew this was the first place we'd go into together. I always
got scared as soon as the decision was made, though it never
took long for fright to get chased off as I tried to fathom a way
into the joint.

I told Doris: 'You go to the end of the street and keep conk.
I'll try to force this gate, and whistle if I do. If you see anybody
coming walk back here, and we'll cuddle up as if we're
courting.' She did as she was told, while I got to work on the
gate lock, using first the bottle-opener and then the nail-file,
then the spike. With a bit more play it snapped back, and I
whistled. We were in the yard.

There was no word said from beginning to end. If I'd been
doing it with a mate you'd have heard scufflings and mutter-
ings, door-rattlings and shoulder-knocks and the next thing
we'd be in a cop car on our way to Guildhall. But now, our
limbs and eyes acted together, as if controlled by one person
that was neither of us, a sensation I'd never known before. A
side door opened and we went between a line of machines
into a partitioned office to begin a quiet and orderly search.
I'd been once in a similar place with a pal, and the noise as we
pulled drawers and slung typewriters about, and took pot
shots with elastic and paperclips at light bulbs was so insane
that it made me stop and silence him as well after five minutes.
But now there wasn't a scratch or click anywhere.

Still with no word I walked to the door, and Doris came
after me. In two seconds we were back on the street, leaning
against the workshop wall to fill each of our mouths with
such kisses that I knew I loved her, and that from then on I
was in the fire, floating, burning, feeling the two of us ready

to explode if we didn't get out of this to where we could lie down. Nothing would stop us, because we already matched and fused together, not even if we fell into a river or snow-bank.

There was no gunning of feet from the factory so that a lawful passing pedestrian could suspect we were up to no good and squeal for the coppers. After five minutes snogging we walked off, as if we'd just noticed how late it was and remembered we had to be at work in the morning. At the main road I said: 'What did you get?'

She took a bundle of pound notes from her pocket: 'This. What about you?'

I emptied a large envelope of postage stamps and cheques: 'Useless. You got the kitty, then.'

'I guess so,' she said, not sounding too full of joy.

'Not bad for a beginner. A school kid, as well!' I gave her half the stamps and she handed me half the money—which came to twenty quid apiece. We homed our way the couple of miles back, sticking one or two stamps (upside down) on each of the corners turned. 'I don't write letters,' I laughed. It was a loony action, but I have to do something insane on every job, otherwise there's no chance of getting caught, and if there's no chance of getting caught, there's no chance of getting away. I explained this to Doris, who said she'd never heard such a screwy idea, but that she was nearly convinced about it because I was more experienced than she was. Luckily the stamps ran out, otherwise the trail would have gone right through our back door, up the stairs and into my bedroom, the last one on my pillow hidden by my stupid big head. I felt feather-brained and obstinate, knowing that even if the world rolled over me I wouldn't squash.

By the banks of the Leen at Bobber's Mill we got under the fence and went down where nobody could see us. It was after midnight, and quiet but for the sound of softly rolling cold water a few feet off, as black as heaven for the loving we had to do.

Doris called for me at home, turned the corner, and came down our cobbled street on a horse. My brother Paul ran in and said:

'Come and look at this woman (he was only nine) on a horse, our Tony'—and having nothing better to do while waiting for Doris but flip through the *Mirror* I strode to the yard-end. It was a warm day, dust in the wind making a lazy atmosphere around the eyes, smoke sneaking off at right angles to chimneys and telly masts. By the pavement I looked down the street and saw nothing but a man going across to the shop in shirtsleeves and braces, then swivelling my eyes the other way I saw this girl coming down the street on a walking horse.

It was a rare sight, because she was beautiful, had blonde hair like Lady Godiva except that she was dressed in riding slacks and a white shirt that set a couple of my Ted mates whistling at her, though most stayed quiet with surprise—and envy—when the horse pulled up at our yard-end and Doris on it said hello to me. It was hard to believe that last night we'd broken into a factory, seemed even more far gone than in a dream; though what we'd done later by the river was real enough, especially when I caught that smell of scent and freshness as she bent down from the horse's neck. 'Why don't you come in for a cup of tea? Bring your horse in for a crust as well.'

It was a good filly, the colour of best bitter, with eyes like priceless damsons that were alive because of the reflector-light in them. The only horses seen on our street—pulling coal carts or bread vans—had gone to the knackers' yards years ago. I took the bridle and led it up the yard, Doris talking softly from high up and calling it Marian, guiding it over the smooth stones. A man came out of a lavatory and had a fit in his eyes when he nearly bumped into it. 'It wain't bite you, George,' I laughed.

'I'll have it for Sunday dinner if it does,' he said, stalking off.

'It wain't be the first time,' I called. My mother was washing clothes at the scullery sink, and it pushed its head to the window for a good look—until she glanced up: 'Tony! What have you got there!'

'Only a horse, mam,' I shouted back. 'It's all right: I ain't nicked it'—as she came out drying her hands.

'A friend of mine come to see me,' I told her, introducing

Doris, who dropped to her proper size on the ashphalt. My mother patted the horse as if it were a stray dog, then went in for a piece of bread. She'd been brought up in the country, and liked animals.

'We had a good time last night,' I said to Doris, thinking about it.

'Not bad. What shall we do with the money?'

'Spend it.'

Our fence was rickety, looked as if it would fall down when she tethered the horse to it. 'Funny,' she said. 'But what on?'

'How much does a horse cost?' I asked, tapping its nose.

'I'm not sure. Dad got me Marian. More than twenty pounds, though.' I was disappointed, had pictured us riding in the country, overland to Langley Mill and Matlock Bath without using a road once, the pair of us making a fine silhouette on some lonely skyline. Then as on the films we'd wind our way far down into the valley and get lodgings at a pub or farmhouse. Bit by bit we'd edge to Scotland and maybe at the end of all our long wanderings by horse we'd get a job as man and wife working a lighthouse. Set on a rock far out at sea, the waves would bash at it like mountains of snow, and we'd keep the lights going, still loving each other and happy even though we hadn't had a letter or lettuce in six months.

The sun shone over our backyards, and I was happy anyway: 'I'll just get rid of my dough, enjoy myself. I'm out of work, so it'll keep me for a month.'

'I hope we don't have to wait that long before doing it again,' she said, brushing her hair back.

'We'll go tonight, if you like. I'll bet the coppers don't know we went into that factory yet.' My mother came out with a bag of crusts for the horse: 'I've just made a pot of tea,' she said. 'Go and pour it, Tony.'

When we got behind the door I pulled Doris to me and kissed her. She kissed me, as well. Not having to chase and fight for it made it seem like real love.

We went on many 'expeditions', as Doris called them. I even got a makeshift job at a factory in case anybody should wonder how I was living. Doris asked if it would be O.K. to bring a school pal with us one night, and this caused our first argument. I said she was loony to think of such a thing, and did she imagine I was running a school for cowing crime, or summat? I hoped she hadn't mentioned our prowling nights to anybody else—though she hadn't, as it turned out, and all she'd wanted was to see if this particular girl at her school would be able to do this sort of job as cool as she could. 'Well, drop it,' I said, sharp. 'We do all right by oursens, so let's keep it to oursens.'

Having been brought up as the ragman's daughter and never wanting for dough, she had hardly played with the kids in the street. She hadn't much to do with those at school either, for they lived mostly in new houses and bungalows up Wollaton and would never come to Radford to call on her. So she'd been lonely in a way I never had been.

Her parents lived in a house off Churchfield Lane, a big ancient one backing its yards (where the old man still kept some of his scrap mountains) on to the Leen. Her dad had worked like a navvy all day and every day of his life, watching each farthing even after he was rich enough to retire like a lord. I don't know what else he could have done. Sucked ice-cream at the seaside? Gardened his feet off? Fished himself to death? He preferred to stick by sun, moon or electric light sorting metal or picking a bone with his own strength because, being a big and satisfied man, that was all he felt like doing—and who could blame him? Doris told me he was mean with most things, though not with her. She could have what she liked.

'Get a hundred, then,' I said.

But she just smiled and thought that wouldn't be right, that she'd only have from him what he gave her because she liked it better that way.

Every week-end she came to our house, on her horse except when the weather was bad. If nobody else was in she fastened her steed to the fence and we went up to my bedroom, got undressed and had the time of our lives. She had a marvellous figure, small breasts for her age, yet wide hips as if they'd finished growing before anything else of her. I always had the idea she felt better out of her clothes, realizing maybe that no clothes, even if expensive like gold, could ever match her birthday suit for a perfect fit that was always the height of fashion. We'd put a few Acker Bilk's low on my record player and listen for a while with nothing on, getting drowsy and warmed up under the usual talk and kisses. Then after having it we'd sit and talk more, maybe have it again before mam or dad shouted up that tea was ready. When on a quiet day the horse shuffled and whinnied, it was like being in a cottage bedroom, alone with her and in the country. If it was sunny and warm as well and a sudden breeze pushed air into the room and flipped a photo of some pop singer off the shelf and fell softly at our bare skins I'd feel like a stallion, as fit and strong as a buck African and we'd have it over and over so that my legs wobbled as I walked back down the stairs.

People got used to seeing her ride down the street, and they'd say: 'Hellow, duck'—adding: 'He's in'—meaning me— 'I just saw him come back from the shop with a loaf.' George Clark asked when I was going to get married, and when I shouted that I didn't know he laughed: 'I expect you've got to find a place big enough for the horse as well, first.' At which I told him to mind his own effing business.

Yet people were glad that Doris rode down our street on a horse, and I sensed that because of it they even looked up to me more—or maybe they only noticed me in a different way to being carted off by the coppers. Doris was pleased when a man coming out of the bookie's called after her: 'Hey up, Lady Luck!'—waving a five-pound note in the air.

Often we'd go down town together, ending up at the pictures, or in a pub over a bitter or babycham. But nobody dreamed what we got up to before finally parting for our different houses. If we pinched fags or food or clothes we'd push what was possible through the letterbox of the first house we came to, or if it was too big we'd leave good things in litter-bins for some poor tramp or tatter to find. We were hardly ever seen, and never caught, on these expeditions, as if love made us invisible, ghosts without sound walking hand in hand between dark streets until we came to some factory, office, lock-up shop or house that we knew was empty of people—and every time this happened I remember the few seconds of surprise, not quite fear, at both of us knowing exactly what to do. I would stand a moment at this surprise—thankful, though waiting for it to go—until she squeezed my hand, and I was moving again, to finish getting in.

I was able to buy a motorbike, a secondhand powerful speedster, and when Doris called she'd leave her horse in our backyard, and we'd nip off for a machine-spin towards Stanton Ironworks, sliding into a full ton once we topped Balloon House Hill and had a few miles of straight and flat laid out for us like an airport runway. Slag heaps looked pale blue in summer, full triangles set like pyramid-targets way ahead and I'd swing towards them between leaf hedges of the country road, hoping they'd keep that far-off vacant colour, as if they weren't real. They never did though, and I lost them at a dip and bend, and when next in sight they were grey and useless and scabby, too real to look good any more.

On my own I rode with L plates, and took a test so as to get rid of them on the law's side of the law, but I didn't pass because I never was good at examinations. Roaring along with Doris straight as goldenrod behind, and hearing noises in the wind tunnel I made whisper sweet nothings into our four ear-holes, was an experience we loved, and I'd shout: 'You can't ride this fast on a horse'—and listen to the laugh she gave, which meant she liked to do both.

She once said: 'Why don't we go on an expedition on your bike?' and I answered: 'Why don't we do one on your hoss?' adding: 'Because it'd spoil everything, wouldn't it?'

She laughed: 'You're cleverer than I think.'

'No kidding,' I said, sarky. 'If only you could see yoursen as I can see you, and if only I could see mysen as you can see me, things would be plainer for us, wouldn't they?'

I couldn't help talking. We'd stopped the bike and were leaning on a bridge wall, with nothing but trees and a narrow lane roundabout, and the green-glass water of a canal below. Her arm was over my shoulder, and my arm was around her waist: 'I wonder if they would?' she said.

'I don't know. Let's go down into them trees.'

'What for?'

'Because I love you.'

She laughed again: 'Is that all?'—then took my arm: 'Come on, then.'

We played a game for a long time in our street, where a gang of us boys held fag lighters in a fair wind, flicking them on and off and seeing which light stayed on longest. It was a stupid game because everything was left to chance, and though this can be thrilling you can't help but lose by it in the end. This game was all the rage for weeks, before we got fed up, or our lighters did, I forget which. Sooner or later every lighter goes out or gives in; or a wind in jackboots jumps from around the corner and kicks it flat—and you get caught under the avalanche of the falling world.

One summer's week-end we waited in a juke-box coffee bar for enough darkness to settle over the streets before setting out. Doris wore jeans and sweatshirt, and I was without a jacket because of the warm night. Also due to the warmth we didn't walk the miles we normally did before nipping into something, which was a pity because a lot of hoof-work put our brains and bodies into tune for such quiet jobs, relaxed and warmed us so that we became like cats, alert and ready at any warning sound to duck or scram. Now and again the noise of the weather hid us—thunder, snow, drizzle, wind, or even the fact that clouds were above made enough noise for us to operate more safely than on this night of open sky with a million ears and eyes of copper stars cocked and staring. Every footstep deafened me, and occasionally on our casual stroll we'd stop to look at each other, stand a few seconds under the wall of a side-lit empty street, then walk on hand in hand. I wanted to whistle (softly) or sing a low tune to myself, for, though I felt uneasy at the open dumb night, it was also the kind of night that left me confident and full of energy, and when these things joined I was apt to get a bit reckless. But I held back, slowed my heart and took in every detail of each same street—so as to miss no opportunity, as they drummed into us at school. 'I feel as if I've had a few,' I said, in spite of my resolution.

'So do I.'

'Or as if we'd just been up in my room and had it together.'

'I don't feel like going far, though,' she said.

'Tired, duck?'

'No, but let's go home. I don't feel like it tonight.'

I wondered what was wrong with her, saying: 'I'll walk you back and we'll call it a day.'

In the next street I saw a gate leading to the rear yard of a shop, and I was too spun up to go home without doing anything at all: 'Let's just nip in here. You needn't come, duck. I wain't be five minutes.'

'O.K.' She smiled, though my face was already set at that loot-barrier. It wasn't very high, and when I was on top she called: 'Give me a hand up.'

'Are you sure?'

'Of course I am.' It was the middle of a short street, and lamp-posts at either end didn't shed radiance this far up. I got to the back door and, in our usual quiet way, the lock was forced and we stood in a smell of leather, polish and cardboard boxes.

'It's a shoe shop,' Doris said. I felt my path across the storehouse behind the selling part of the shop, by racks and racks of shoe boxes, touching paper and balls of string on a corner table.

We went round it like blind people in the dark a couple of times just to be sure we didn't miss a silent cashbox cringing and holding its breath as our fingers went by. People on such jobs often miss thousands through hurrying or thinking the coppers are snorting down their necks. My old man insists I get the sack from one firm after another because I'm not thorough enough in my work, but if he could have seen me on this sort of task he'd have to think again.

There was nothing in the backroom. I went into the shop part and in ten seconds flat was at the till, running my fingers over them little plastic buttons as if I was going to write a letter to my old man explaining just how thorough I could be at times. To make up for the coming small clatter of noise I held my breath—hoping both would average out to make it not heard. A couple of no-good night owls walked by outside, then I turned the handle and felt the till drawer thump itself towards my guts. It's the best punch in the world, like a tabby cat boxing you with its paw, soft and loaded as it slides out on ballbearing rollers.

My hand made the lucky dip, lifted a wad of notes from under a spring-weight, and the other scooped up silver, slid it into my pocket as if it were that cardboard money they used to lend us at infants' school to teach us how to be good shoppers and happy savers—not rattling good coin ready for grown-ups to get rid of. I went to the back room and stood by the exit to make sure all was clear.

The light went on, a brilliant blue striplight flooding every corner of the room. I froze like a frog that's landed in grass instead of water. When I could speak I said to Doris: 'What did you do that for?'—too scared to be raving mad.

'Because I wanted to.' She must have sensed how much I felt like bashing her, because: 'Nobody can see it from the street'—which could have been true, but even so.

'Kicks are kicks,' I said, 'but this is a death trap.'

'Scared?' she smiled.

'Just cool'—feeling anything but. 'I've got about fifty quid in my pocket.'

She stood against a wall of shoe boxes, and even a telly ad couldn't have gone deeper into my guts than the sight of Doris now. Yellow arms of light turned full on her left me in the shade—which was fine, for I expected to see the dead mug of a copper burst in at any moment. Yet even at that I wouldn't be able to care. I felt as if music was in my head wanting to get out, as if it had come to me because I was one of those who could spin it out from me, though knowing I'd never had any say in a thing like that.

She didn't speak, stood to her full fair height and stared. I knew we were safe, that no copper would make any capture that night because the light she had switched on protected us both. We were cast-iron solid in this strong-box of shoes, and

Doris knew it as well because when I couldn't help but smile she broke the spell by saying:

'I want to try some shoes on.'

'What?'

'Maybe they've got some of the latest.'

The idea was barmy, not so that I wanted to run like a shot stag out of the place, but so that I could have done a handstand against the wall of boxes. I lifted out an armful and set them on the floor like a game of dominoes. She chose one and opened it gently. I took up a box and split it down the middle: 'Try these.'

They were too small, a pair of black shiners with heels like toothpicks. 'I wish the shopkeeper was here,' she said, 'then he could tell me where the best are. This is a waste of time.'

I scoffed. 'You don't want much, do you? You'd have to pay for them, then. No, we'll go through the lot and find a few pairs of Paris fashions.'

'Not in this shop'—contemptuously slinging a pair of plain lace-ups to the other side of the room, enough noise to wake every rat under the skirting board. From the ladder I passed down a few choice boxes, selecting every other on the off chance of picking winners. 'I should have come in skirt and stockings,' she said, 'then I could have told which ones suit me.'

'Well, next time we go into a shoe shop I'll let you know; I'll wear an evening suit and we'll bring a transistor to do a hop with. Try these square toes. They'll go well with slacks.'

They fitted but, being the wrong colour, were hurled out with the other misfits. The room was scattered with shoes, looked as if one of them Yank cyclones—Mabel or Edna or whatever you call them—had been hatched there, or as if a meeting of cripples and one-legs had been suddenly broken up by news of the four-minute warning. She still hadn't found the right pair, so went on looking as if she lived there, ordering shop-assistant me about, though I didn't mind because it seemed like a game we were playing. 'Why don't you find a pair for yourself?' she said.

'No, we'll get you fixed. I'm always well shod.'

I knew that we were no longer safe in that shop and sprang to switch off the lights. 'You silly fool,' she cried.

Darkness put us into another world, the real one we were used to, or that I was anyway because it was hard to tell which sort of world Doris felt at home in. All she wanted, I sometimes thought, was a world with kicks, but I didn't fancy being for long at the mercy of a world in pitboots. Maybe it wore carpet slippers when dealing with her—though I shouldn't get like that now that it's been over for so long.

'Why did you switch off the light?' she yelled.

'Come on, let's get outside.'

We were in the yard, Doris without any pair of shoes except those she'd come out in that evening. The skyline for me ended at the top of the gate, for a copper was coming over it, a blue-black tree trunk bending towards us about twenty yards away. Doris was frozen like a rabbit. I pushed her towards some back sheds so that she was hidden between two of them before the copper, now in the yard, spotted the commotion.

He saw me, though. I dodged to another space, then ricochetted to the safe end of the yard, and when he ran at me, stinking of fags and beer, I made a nip out of his long arms and was on the gate saddle before he could reach me.

'Stop, you little bogger,' he called. 'I've got you.'

But all he had was one of my feet, and after a bit of tugging I left my shoe in the copper's hand. As I was racing clippitty-clop, hop-skip-and-a-jump up the street, I heard his boots rattling the boards of the gate as he got over—not, thank God, having twigged that Doris was in there and could now skip free.

I was a machine, legs fastened to my body like nuts and bolts, arms pulling me along as I ran down that empty street. I turned each corner like a flashing tadpole, heart in my head as I rattled the pavement so fast that I went from the eye of lamp-post in what seemed like no seconds at all. There was no worry in my head except the need to put a mile of zig-zags between that copper and me. I'd stopped hearing him only a few yards from the shoe shop gate, but it seemed that half an hour passed before I had to give up running in case I blew to pieces from the heavy bombs now getting harder all over me.

Making noises like a crazy elephant, I walked, only realising now that one of my shoes was missing. The night had fallen apart, split me and Doris from each other, and I hoped she'd made a getaway before the copper gave me up and went back to check on what I'd nicked.

I threw my other shoe over the wall of an old chapel and went home barefoot, meaning to buy myself some more next day with the fifty quid still stuck in my pocket. The shoe landed on a heap of cinders and rusting cans, and the softness of my feet on the pavement was more than made up for by the solid ringing curses my brain and heart played ping-pong with. I kept telling myself this was the end, and though I knew it was, another voice kept urging me to hope for the best and look on the bright side—like some mad deceiving parson on the telly.

I was so sure of the end that before turning into our street I dropped the fifty pound bundle through somebody's letter box and hoped that when they found it they'd not say a word to anybody about such good luck. This in fact was what happened, and by the time I was safe for a three-year lap in borstal the old woman who lived there had had an unexpected good time on the money that was, so she said, sent to her by a grateful and everloving nephew in Sheffield.

Next morning two cops came to our door, and I knew it was no good lying because they looked at me hard, as if they'd seen me on last night's television reading the news. One of them held my shoes in his hand: 'Do these fit you?'

A short while before my capture Doris said, when we were kissing good night outside her front door: 'I've learnt a lot since meeting you. I'm not the same person any more.' Before I had time to find out what she'd learnt I was down at the cop shop and more than half-way to borstal. It was a joke, and I laughed on my way there. They never knew about Doris, so she went scot-free, riding her horse whenever she felt like it.

I had that to be glad about at least. As a picture it made a stove in my guts those first black months, and as a joke I laughed over and over again, because it would never go stale on me. I'd learned a lot as well since meeting Doris, though to be honest I even now can't explain what it is. But what I learned is still in me, feeding my quieter life with energy almost without my noticing it.

I wrote to Doris from borstal but never received an answer, and even my mother couldn't tell me anything about her, or maybe wouldn't, because plenty happened to Doris that all the district knew of. Myself though, I was kept three years in the dark, suffering and going off my head at something that without this love and worry I'd have sailed through laughing. Twenty of the lads would jump on me when I raved at night, and gradually I became low and brainless and without breath like a beetle and almost stopped thinking of her, hoping that maybe she'd be waiting for me when I came out and that we'd be able to get married.

That was the hope of story books, of television and BBC; didn't belong at all to me and life and somebody like Doris. For three solid years my brain wouldn't leave me alone, came at me each night and rolled over me like a wheel of fire, so that I still sweat blood at the thought of that torture, waiting, without news, like a dwarf locked in the dark. No borstal could take the credit for such punishment as this.

On coming out I pieced everything together. Doris had been pregnant when I was sent down, and three months later married a garage mechanic who had a reputation for flying around on motorbikes like a dangerous loon. Maybe that was how she prolonged the bout of kicks that had started with me, but this time it didn't turn out so well. The baby was a boy, and she named it after me. When it was two months old she went out at Christmas Eve with her husband. They were going to a dance at Derby on the motorbike and, tonning around a frosty bend, met a petrol bowser side on. Frost, darkness, and large red letters spelling PETROL were the last things she saw, and I wondered what was in her mind at that moment. Not much, because she was dead when the bowser man found her, and so was her husband. She couldn't have been much over eighteen.

'It just about killed her dad as well,' my mother said, 'broke his heart. I talked to him once on the street, and he said he'd allus wanted to send her to the university, she was so clever. Still, the baby went back to him.'

And I went back to jail, for six months, because I opened a car door and took out a transistor radio. I don't know why I did it. The wireless was no good to me and I didn't need it. I wasn't even short of money. I just opened the car door and took out the radio and, here's what still mystifies me, I switched it on straightaway and listened to some music as I walked down the street, so that the bloke who owned the car heard it and chased after me.

But that was the last time I was in the nick—touch wood—and maybe I had to go in, because when I came out I was able to face things again, walk the streets without falling under a bus or smashing a jeweller's window for the relief of getting caught.

I got work at a sawmill, keeping the machines free of dust and wood splinters. The screaming engine noise ripping through trunks and planks was even fiercer than the battle-shindig in myself, which was a good thing during the first months I was free. I rode there each morning on a new-bought bike, to work hard before eating my dinner sandwiches under a spreading chestnut tree. The smell of fresh leaves on the one hand, and newly flying sawdust on the other, cleared my head and made me feel part of the world again. I liked it so much I thought it was the best job I'd ever had—even though the hours were long and the wages rotten.

One day I saw an elderly man walking through the wood, followed by a little boy who ran in and out of the bushes whacking flowers with his stick. The kid was about four, dressed in cowboy suit and hat, the other hand firing off his six-shooter that made midget sharp cracks splitting like invisible twigs between the trees. He was pink-faced with grey eyes, the terror of cats and birds, a pest for the ice-cream man, the sort of kid half stunned by an avalanche of toys at

Christmas, spoiled beyond recall by people with money. You could see it in his face.

I got a goz at the man, had to stare a bit before I saw it was Doris's father, the scrap merchant who'd not so long back been the menace of the street in his overdriven car. He was grey and wax in the face, well wrapped in topcoat and hat and scarf and treading carefully along the woodpath. 'Come on,' he said to the kid. 'Come on, Tony, or you'll get lost.'

I watched him run towards the old man, take his hand and say: 'Are we going home now, grandad?' I had an impulse, which makes me blush to remember it, and that was to go up to Doris's ragman father and say—what I've already said in most of this story, to say that in a way he was my father as well, to say: 'Hey up, dad. You don't know much, do you?' But I didn't, because I couldn't, leaned against a tree, feeling as if I'd done a week's work without stop, feeling a hundred years older than that old man who was walking off with my kid.

My last real sight of Doris was of her inside the shoe shop trying on shoes, and after that, when I switched off the light because I sensed danger, we both went into the dark, and never came out. But there's another and final picture of her that haunts me like a vision in my waking dreams. I see her coming down the street, all clean and golden-haired on that shining horse, riding it slowly towards our house to call on me, as she did for a long time. And she was known to men standing by the bookies as Lady Luck.

That's a long while ago, and I even see Doris's kid, a big lad now, running home from school. I can watch him without wanting to put my head in the gas oven, watch him and laugh to myself because I was happy to see him at all. He's in good hands and prospering. I'm going straight as well, working in the warehouse where they store butter and cheese. I eat like a fighting cock, and take home so much that my wife and two kids don't do bad on it either.

THE OTHER JOHN PEEL

When the world was asleep one Sunday morning Bob slid away from the warm aura of his wife and padded downstairs—boots in hand—to fix up a flask and some bacon sandwiches.

Electric light gave the living-room an ageless air, only different from last night in that it was empty—of people. He looked around at the house full of furniture: television set, washing machine glinting white from the scullery, even a car on the street—the lot, and it belonged to him. Eric and Freda also slept, and he'd promised to take them up the Trent and hire a rowing-boat this afternoon if they were good. Wearing his second-best suit, knapsack all set, he remembered Freda's plea a few days ago: 'Will you bring me one o' them tails, our dad?' He had to laugh, the fawce little bogger, as he combed his dark wavy hair at the mirror and put on his glasses. I must tell her not to blab it to her pals though.

He opened the cellar door for his guns and pouches, put them under his arm to keep them low—having a licence for the twelve-bore, but not the .303 service rifle—and went out into the backyard. The world was a cemetery on short lease to the night, dead quiet except for the whine of factory generators: a row of upstairs windows were closed tight to hold in the breath of sleep. A pale grey saloon stood by the kerb, the best of several left out on the cobbles, and Bob stowed his guns well down behind the back seat before lighting a cigarette.

The streets were yours at six on a Sunday morning, flying through the cradle of a deadbeat world with nothing to stop you getting what fun and excitement you wanted. The one drawback to the .303 was that out of fifty bullets from the army he'd but twenty left, though if he rationed himself to a shot every Sunday there'd still be six months' sport for the taking. And you never knew: maybe he could tap his cousin in the terriers for a belt of souvenirs.

He bounded through the traffic lights, between church and pub, climbing the smooth tarmac up Mansfield Road, then pouring his headlights into the dip and heading north under a sky of stars. Houses fell endlessly back on either side, a gauntlet trying to cup him but getting nowhere. The wireless had forecast a fine day and looked like being right for a change, which was the least they could do for you. It was good to get out after a week cooped-up, to be a long-range hunter in a car that blended with the lanes. He was doing well for himself: wife and kids, a good toolsetting job, and a four-roomed house at fifteen bob a week. Fine. And most Sunday mornings he ranged from Yorkshire to Lincolnshire, and Staffordshire to Leicestershire, every map-point a sitting duck for his coolly sighted guns.

On the dot of six-thirty he saw Ernie by the Valley Road picture house. 'Hey up,' Ernie said as he pulled in. 'That was well timed.' Almost a foot taller than Bob, he loomed over the car dressed in an old mac.

'It's going to be fine,' Bob said, 'according to the radio.'

Ernie let himself in. 'The wireless's allus wrong. Spouts nowt but lies. I got welloes on in case it rains.'

They scooted up the dual carriageway. 'Is this the best you can do?' Ernie asked. 'You can fetch ninety out of this, I'm sure. 'Ark at that engine: purring like a she-cat on the batter.'

'Take your sweat,' Bob said. 'This is a mystery trip.'

Ernie agreed. 'I'm glad there's no racing on a Sunday. It's good to get out a bit like this.'

'It is, an' all. Missis well?'

'Not too bad. Says she feels like a battleship with such a big belly'—and went silent. Bob knew him well enough: he'd never talk just to be friendly; they could drive for an hour and he'd stay shut, often in an icy far-off mood that didn't give him anything to say or think of. They worked a dozen feet from each other all week, Bob on his precision jobs, Ernie watching a row of crankshift millers. 'What guns you got then?' he asked.

Bob peered ahead, a calm and measured glance along the lit-up wastes of the road to Ollerton. 'A twelve-bore and a ·303.'

'I wish you had,' Ernie laughed. 'You never know when you're going to need a ·303 these days. Best gun out.'

'Keep your trap shut about it though,' Bob said. 'I got it in the army. I wouldn't tell you except that I know I can trust you by now.'

Maybe he wasn't joking, Ernie thought. Bob was clever with hands and brain, the stop-gap of the shop with micrometer and centre-lathe, a toolmaker who could turn off a candlestick or fag-lighter as soon as look at you. 'Do you mean it about a ·303?'

Bob pulled into a lay-by and got out. 'Keep clear of the headlights,' he said, 'but catch this.' Ernie caught it, pushed forward the safety catch, the magazine resting in the net of his fingers. 'God Almighty! Anything up the spout?'

'I've a clip in my pocket. Strictly for rabbits'—Bob smiled, taking it back.

'A waste,' Ernie said. 'The twelve-bore would do. Mixermatosis has killed 'em all off, anyway.'

They drove on. 'Had it since I left the army,' Bob told him. 'The stores was in a chronic state in Germany at the end of the war. Found myself with two, so kept one. I have a pot-shot with it now and again. I enjoy hunting—for a bit o' recreation.'

Ernie laughed, wildly and uncontrolled, jerking excited shouts into the air as if trying to throw something out of his mouth, holding his stomach to stop himself doubling up, wearing down the shock of what a free-lance ·303 meant. He put his arm around Bob's shoulder by way of congratulation: 'You'd better not let many people know about it, or the coppers'll get on to you.'

'Don't worry. If ever they search, it's a souvenir. I'd get rid of the bolt, and turn another off on the lathe when I needed it.'

'Marvellous,' Ernie said. 'A ·303! Just the thing to have in case of a revolution. I hope I can get my hands on one when the trouble starts.'

Bob was sardonic: 'You and your revolution! There wain't be one in our lifetimes, I can tell you that.' Ernie had talked revolution to him for months, had argued with fiery puritanical force, guiding Bob's opinion from voting Labour to a head-nodding acceptance of rough and ready Communism. 'I can't see why you think there'll be a revolution though.'

'I've told you though,' Ernie said loudly. 'There's got to be something. I feel it. We wok in a factory, don't we? Well, we're the backbone of the country, but you see, Bob, there's too many people on our backs. And it's about time they was slung off. The last strike we had a bloke in a pub said to me: "Why are you fellows allus on strike?" And I said to 'im: "What sort o' wok do you do?" And he said: "I'm a travelling salesman." So I said, ready to smash 'im: "Well, the reason I come out on strike is because I want to get bastards like yo' off my back." That shut 'im up. He just crawled back into his sherry.'

At dawn they stopped the car in a ladle of land between Tuxford and the Dukeries, pulling on to a grass verge by a gate. A tall hawthorn hedge covered in green shoots bordered the lane, and the bosom of the meadow within rose steeply to a dark skyline, heavy rolls of cloud across it. Ernie stood by the gate: 'The clouds smell fresh'—pulling his mac collar up. 'Think we'll get owt 'ere?'

'It's good hunting country' Bob told him. 'I know for a fact.'

They opened flasks and tore hungrily into sandwiches. 'Here, have a swig of this,' Ernie said, pouring some into his own cup. 'It'll do you good.'

Bob held it to the light. 'What is it?'

'Turps and dash. Here's the skin off your lips.'

'Don't talk so loud. You'll chase all the wild life away. Not a bad drop, is it?'

'A rabbit wouldn't get far with a ·303 at its arse.' A sort of loving excitement paralysed his fingers when he picked up the rifle: 'Can you get me one?'

'They don't grow on trees, Ernie.'

'I'd like one, though. For the next war. I'd just wait for

somebody to try and call me up!' They leaned on the gate, smoking. 'Christ, when the Russians come I'll be liberated.'

'It's a good job everybody ain't like you,' Bob said with a smile. 'You're a rare 'un, yo' are.'

Ernie saw a movement across the field, beginning from the right and parting a diagonal line of grass, ascending towards the crest on their left. The light from behind showed it up clear and neat. 'See it?' he hissed, ramming a shell in the twelve-bore. Bob said nothing, noiselessly lifted the ·303. No need to use that, Ernie thought. It'd bring a man down a mile off; a twelve-bore's good enough for a skinful of mixer-matosis.

A sudden wind blew against the dawn, ruffling the line of their prey. Bob's eye was still on it: a single round went into the breech. 'I'll take it,' he said softly. It was already out of buck-shot from Ernie's twelve-bore. Both lost it, but said nothing. A lull in the wind didn't show it up. 'I expect it's a hare.'

Bob lowered his ·303, but Ernie signalled him to be quiet: it seemed as if a match were lit in the middle of the field, a slow-burning brown flame moving cautiously through shallow grass, more erratic now, but still edging towards the crest. The cold, star-flecked sky needed only a slow half turn to bring full daylight. What the bloody hell is it? Ernie wondered. Fields and lane were dead quiet: they were kings of the countryside: no houses, no one in sight. He strained his eyes hoping to discover what it was. A squirrel? Some gingernut, anyway.

A smile came on to Bob's face, as when occasionally at work his patience paid off over some exacting job, a flange going into place with not half a thou' to spare. Now it was more heightened than that: a triumph of hunting. Two sharp ears were seen on the skyline, a hang-dog tail, a vulpine mouth breakfasting on wind—with Ernie's heart a bongo drum playing rhythms on his chest wall: A fox.

The air split open, and from all directions came a tidal wave of noise, rushing in on every ear but that to which the bullet had been aimed. Together they were over the gate, and speeding up the slope as if in a dawn attack. Gasping, Bob knelt and turned the dead fox over: as precise a job as he had ever done. 'I always get 'em in the head if I can. I promised one of the tails to a neighbour.'

'Ain't this the first fox you've shot, then?' Ernie couldn't fathom his quiet talk: a fox stone-dead from a ·303 happened once in a lifetime. They walked down the hill. 'I've had about half a dozen,' he said by the car door, dragging a large poly-thene bag from under the seat and stuffing the dead fox into it. 'From round here most on 'em. I'll knock off a bit and go to Lincolnshire next time.' The fox lay as if under a glass case, head bashed and tail without colour. 'It never stood a chance with a ·303,' Ernie grinned.

He took the wheel going back, flying down lanes to the main road, setting its nose at Mansfield as if intent on cutting Nottinghamshire in two. Bob lounged behind using a pull-through on the ·303. 'I've allus liked hunting,' he shouted to Ernie. 'My old man used to go poaching before the war, so we could have summat to eat. He once did a month in quod, the poor bastard. Never got a chance to enjoy real hunting, like me.'

'I want the next tail, for the kid that's coming,' Ernie said, laughing.

Bob was pleased with himself: 'You talk about revolution: the nobs around here would go daft if they knew I was knocking their sport off.'

It was broad daylight: 'Have another turps and dash,' Ernie said, 'you clever bleeder. You'll find the bottle in my haversack.'

The road opened along a high flat ridge through a colliery village, whose grey houses still had no smoke at their chimneys. Silent headstocks to the left towered above the fenced-off coppices of Sherwood Forest.

THE FIREBUG

I smile as much as feel ashamed at the memory of some of the things I did when I was a lad, even though I caused my mother a lot of trouble. I used to pinch her matches and set fire to heaps of paper and anything I could get my eyes on.

I was no bigger than sixpenorth o' coppers, so's you'd think I wasn't capable of harming a fly. People came straight out with it: 'Poor little bogger. Butter wouldn't melt in his mouth.' But my auntie used to say: 'He might not be so daft as he looks when he grows up'—and she was right, I can see that now. Her husband had a few brains as well: 'He's quiet, nobody can deny it,' but still waters run deep. I wouldn't trust him an inch.' At this the rest of the family got on to him and called him bully with neither sense nor feeling, said I was delicate and might not have long for this world—while I went on eating my way through a fistful of bread-and-jam as if I hadn't heard a dickybird and would last forever.

This match craze must have started when, still in leggings, I was traipsed downtown by my mother one day midweek. The streets weren't all that crowded and I held on to her carrier-bag, dragging a bit I should think, slurring my other hand along the cold glass of shop windows full of tricycles and forts for Christmas that I would never get—unless they were given to me as a reward for being good enough not to pinch 'em. As usual my mother was harassed to death (on her way to ask for a bit more time to pay off the arrears of 24 Slum Yard I shouldn't wonder) and I was grizzling because I couldn't share as much as I'd have liked in the razzle-dazzle of the downtown street.

Suddenly I left off moaning, felt the air go quiet and blue, as if a streak of sly lightning had stiffened everybody dead in their tracks. Even motor cars stopped. 'What's up, mam?' I said—or whined I expect, because I could only whine up to fourteen: then I went to work and started talking clear and proper, from shock.

Before she could tell me, a bloody great bell began clanging —louder than any school or church call—bowling its ding-dong from every place at once, so that I looked quickly at the up-windows to wonder where it was coming from. I felt myself going white, knees quaking. Not that I was terrified. I was right in the middle of another world, as if the one and only door to it had a bell on saying PRESS, and somebody was leaning his elbow spot-on and drilling right into my startled brain.

The bells got louder, so's I couldn't any longer hope it was only the cops or an ambulance. It was something I'd never seen before nor dreamt of either: a flying red-faced monster batting along the narrow street at a flat-out sixty, as if it had been thrown there like a toy. Only this weighed a ton or two and made the ground shake under me, like a procession for the Coronation or something—but coming at top speed, as if a couple of Russian tanks were after its guts and shooting fire behind. 'What is it, mam? What is it?' I whined when it got quiet enough to speak.

'Only a fire,' she told me. 'A house is on fire, and they're fire-engines going to put it out.' Then another couple of engines came belting through the deadened street, both together it seemed, turning all the air into terrifying klaxons. I started screaming, and didn't stop until I'd gone down in a fit.

Mam and a man carried me into the nearest shop and when I woke up there was nothing but toys all around, so's I thought I was in heaven. To keep me calm the shopkeeper gave me a lead soldier which I was glad to grab, though I'd rather have had the toy fire-engine that caught at my sight as soon as I stood up. It was as if my eyes had opened for the first time since I was born: red with yellow ladders and blue men in helmets—but he turned me away to ask if I was all right, and when I nodded walked me back into the street out of temptation. I was a bit of a bogger in them days.

The long school holidays of summer seemed to go on for

years. When I could scrounge fourpence I'd nip to the continuous downtown pictures after dinner and drop myself in one of the front seats, to see the same film over and over till driven out by hunger or God save the king. But I didn't often get money to go, and now and again mam would bundle me into the street so's her nerves could have a rest from my 'give-me-this-and-I-want-that' sort of grizzling. I'd be quite happy—after the shock of being slung out had worn off—to sit on the pavement making wrinkles in the hot tar with a spoon I'd managed to grab on my way through the kitchen, or drawing patterns with a piece of slate or matchstick. Other kids would be rolling marbles or running at rounders, or a string of them would scream out of an entry after playing hide and seek in somebody's backyard. A few would be away at seaside camp, or out in the fields and woods on Sunday treats, so it worn't as noisy as it might have been. I remember once I sat dead quiet all afternoon doing nothing but talk to myself for minutes at a time on what had happened to me in the last day or two and about things I hoped to do as soon as I got either money or matches in my fist—chuntering ten to the dozen as if somebody unknown to me had put a penny in the gramophone of my brain as they walked by. Other people passing looked at me gone-out, but I didn't give a bogger and just went on talking until the noise of a fire-engine in the distance came through to my locked-in world.

It sounded like a gale just starting up, an aeroplane of bells going along at ground level with folded wings, about ten streets off but far enough away to seem as if it was in another town behind the big white clouds of summer, circling round a dream I'd had about a fire a few nights ago. It didn't sound real, though I knew what it meant now, after my downtown fit a long time back in the winter. Hot sun and empty sky stopped it being loud I suppose, but my heart nearly fell over itself at the brass-band rattle, it went so fast—sitting in my mouth like a cough-drop or dollymixture getting bigger as the bells went on. Most of the other kids ran hollering to where the noise came from, even when I thought they were too far off for anybody else to hear, went clobbering up the street and round a corner until everywhere was quiet and empty except the bells now reaching louder all the time.

I wanted to join in the chase, fly towards fire and smoke as fast as my oversize wellingtons would take me, to see all them helmetted men with hatchets and ladders and hosepipes trying to stop the red flames but not managing so that the only thing left was a couple of cinders one on top of the other. And then I'd try to sneak up and blow the top one off. But I'd never be able to catch them, that much I knew as sure as God made little apples, so I waited till my face changed back from white to mucky and my blood stopped bumping, and went on playing tar games in the sun.

But sometimes I'd sit and hear the bells of a fire engine that none of the other kids would hear, would leave off playing and listen hard for it to come closer, hoping to see one swivel around the bend at the top of our street and pour down with its big nose getting closer—and if it did I wouldn't know whether to stick by and see what happened or run screaming in to mam and get her to hide me under the stairs. I was always hoping for a sweltering fire close by so that I could watch them trying to put it out—hope for one at the bike factory or pub or in some shop or other. But I just heard them now and again in my mind, sat (before I cottoned on to this) waiting for the others to hear it and run yelling to where it come from, but they didn't and then I knew it was just in me the bells had played. This was only on summer days though, as if the sun melted wax in my tabs and let me hear better than anybody else—even things that didn't happen at all.

But fire-engine fires were rare as five-pound notes, and up to then the nearest a big blaze ever came to our street was on bonfire night. They told us about Bonfire Night at school, about how this poor bloke Guy Fawkes got chucked on a fire because he wanted to blow up parliament, and I learned as well about the Great Fire of London where all the town got lit because everything was built of wood. What a sight that must have been! Thousands and thousands of houses going up like matchboxes. Still, I didn't like to think of people getting burnt to death, I do know that. I was terrified on it, and so was dad, and though he used to poke the fire cold out every night, and pull the rugs a long way back from the grate and set the chairs under the window, I was still worried in bed later in case a hot coal lit up again and walked to right across the room where the rugs were; or that somebody next door would go to sleep with his pipe lit and the first thing I'd know was a rubber hose slooshing water through the window and onto us four kids. I wouldn't even have heard the ding-dong-belling of the fire-engine I slept so deep—and that would have broken my heart.

On Bonfire Night fires were lit like cherry trees, two or three to a long street like ours, and the only thing I ever prayed for was that it wouldn't rain after the bigger lads got busy and set their matches under piles of mattresses, boxes and old sofas. The flames climbed so high by ten that house walls glowed and shone as if somebody had scrubbed them clean, and I used to go from one fire-hill to another eating my bread and jam and jumping out of the way when firecrackers got close. I was so excited the bread almost wouldn't go down, and my breath gulped as the warmth tried to ram itself through my throat when I went too near the fire.

If only flames like this blazed all winter, was my one big wish. But they didn't, my brain told me: they flared for one night, hands of fire waving hello and good-bye while we shouted and danced, then died to a glowing hump of grey ash for corporation carts to clear away like the bodies of big runover dogs next morning. Christmas was a letdown after these mountainous fires.

This Bonfire Night I stayed out till twelve hoping, now that everybody else had gone, for a last-minute flame to shoot up for one second and show its face only to me; but all that remained was the smell of fire-ash and gunpowder. Then in the dead quietness I heard the bell of a far-off fire-engine, flying down some empty street with bells full on, passing houses that were so quiet you might think God had gone before and like some fat publican shouted TIME in each. I looked at the fire again in the hope that it would flare and bring the distant engine to where I was, frightened a bit at the same time

43

because I was on my own and would have nobody to stand with if it did. All I got for my waiting though was a spot of ice-cold rain on my arm, and the sound of another big drop burying itself with a hiss chock in the middle of the ash. And the fire-engine went tingling on till I couldn't hear it no more, off to some street where, I thought, they had a bigger fire than could ever be built in ours.

My first fires were nothing to speak of: baby ones built in the backyard with a single sheet of paper that burned out in half a second like celluloid, scattering like black butterflies at the draught of another kid. Mam clouted my tab-hole and took the matches off me—to begin with—but realising after a while how it kept me occupied at a time when she was hard-up for peace and quiet she let me play: a couple of old newspapers and half a dozen matches stopped me whining for an hour, which was cheap at the price. For mam was badly right enough, holding her heart all the time and blue in the face when any-thing harassed her, so that even if I'd wanted to make a row dad would have thumped me one.

So nobody bothered me and my midget fires, because they could see I wasn't doing no harm. One or two of the nosey parkers went as far as to tut-tut loud when they looked over the fence in passing and saw wisps of smoke floating in front of my eyes, but they soon got used to the sight of it and stopped pulling meagrims. They must have known mam knew I'd got the matches, and didn't want a row with her because she was still a wild fighter badly or not. I soon stopped making fires outside our back door, though, because one day I collected a whole tin of matchsticks off the street and they burnt so long in a bad wind that when mam smelled them up in the bedroom dad kicked the fire out with his boots and locked the gate on me. I'd only got a couple o' matches left, and had forgotten to snatch up the newspaper when dad's fist lifted me, so I was feeling hard done by as I sulked near the yard lavatories.

At the first nip of a cold rainspot I went into the nearest because if there was one thing I didn't like it was getting wet. It made me feel so miserable I could have put my head in the gas-oven or gone to the railway line and played with an express till I was bumped into, rolled over, and blacked-out for good. Whenever a spot of rain fell I sheltered in a shop doorway or entry until it stopped even if I was there for hours, because when rain landed on me it was like a shock of pins and needles sending me off my nut, as if every bit of me was a funny bone. And big rain was worse than ever, for it seemed to stick into me like falling penknives.

If I hadn't opened the door and gone in to get out of the rain I'd never have noticed the wad of newspapers stuffed behind the lavatory pipe. Two or three thick Sunday ones, the sort I liked because they'd got bigger letters on the front page than any. Once at Aunt Ethel's one of my grown-up cousins was reading the Sunday paper and his brother put a light to the bottom for a lark, and the other didn't know what was going off till flames reached the terrible headlines and started licking his nose. Or maybe he did, for he stayed as calm as if it had happened before: he was near the range and when the whole paper was in flames just leaned over and let it fall in the firegrate to burn itself out—as if he'd read all he wanted to anyway—and calmly asked his mam if there was any more tea in the pot. I laughed at the thought of it for days and days.

As soon as the heap of papers caught I ran out of the yard and rattled to the bottom of the street, went up to a gang of pals and played marbles so's nobody'd twig anything. I was so excited at what I'd done, and at listening all the time for a fire-engine (that I hoped somebody had called to come rumbling full tilt down the cobbled street with bells ringing), that I lost all my five marbles because I hardly knew what I was doing.

I didn't hear the bells of a fire-engine though: the only ringing that went on was all night in my ears after the old man had given me a good pasting when I went home a long time later. The whole yard talked about my fire-making for days: 'The little varmint wants taming. He's got too much on it.'

'You'd better lock your door when you go over the road

shopping, or he might sneak in and send your home up in flames.'

'If I was his mother I'd take him to have his brains tested, though she can't do a sight at the moment, poor woman. So he gets neglected. I don't know, I don't.'

'He'd be better off at Cumberland Hall,' another woman said—which made me shiver when I heard it because Cumberland Hall's a stark cold place they send kids to as ain't got no mam and dad, where they hit you with sticks, feed you on bread and porridge, and get you up at six in the morning—or so mam once told me when I asked her about it. And it was a long way in the woods, she said, so's I knew if I got sent there I wouldn't be able to hear a fire-engine for years and years. Unless I made a fire on the sly and one had to come and put it out, then I might, but you couldn't depend on it because I knew by now that fire-engines didn't fly ding-donging to every bit of fire in the open air: they had to be big ones, which meant I was beginning to learn. Also I didn't want to get caught again and have my head batted, for as well as it hurting a long time afterwards it might send me daft or dead which would be terrible because then I wouldn't be able to make the fires or hear the engines.

So I knew I'd got to be careful next time and thought about how secret you could be if you did it in a wood and how big a fire it'd grow to if once it got going and the wind blew on it. I dreamed about it for weeks, saw yellow matchlight jump to paper, spread to dry leaves and twigs, climb to dead wood and branches and bushes and little trees and big trees, changing colour from red to blue and green and back to red as the big bell ding-donged through everything, racing from the main road. And all the firemen would just stand there, helmets off and scratching their heads because they wouldn't have a dog's chance of putting it out. I was sweating myself at the thought of it. Once on the pictures I saw where a big oil well caught fire, and they had to have dynamite to put it out. Dynamite! Think of that! Many's the pasting I got from the teacher at school for being half asleep in these daydreams. Once I was called out to the front for it, and as he was holding the strap up

46

to let me have it, the thundery quiet of the classroom was filled with the roar of a fire-engine out on the boulevard. A few seconds went by as everybody wondered where it was going, and I thought the teacher would let me off at such a fire-awful noise, (though I don't know why he should), but the next thing I knew the strap had hit the outstretched palm of my hand as if a large stone had fallen on it from a thousand feet up. The bastard. I should have been listening to him telling us about how the army of some batchy king or other chopped up the senseless blokes of another army; then the two kings shook hands and signed a bit of paper to say things should be the same, but peaceful, and all the soldiers just sat in gangs around their little fires boiling soup and laughing, when all I thought of was how all these little fires could be joined together into a big blaze, as big as a mountain, with the two kings on top instead of that poor bloke called Guy Fawkes—just because he had a funny name.

I went off early one morning, a sunny day one Sunday, all by myself after a breakfast of tomatoes and bacon. Dad was glad to get rid of me because mam was still badly and the doctor was up with her. She hadn't spoken to me for a week because she'd been sleeping most of the time—and all I had to do, dad said, was keep out of her way and then she'd get better quicker.

Well, I was glad to because I'd got other things to brood on, walking down the street well into the wall with a box of matches and some folded paper in my pockets, my hand clutching the matches because I didn't want them to jump out —or fall through the hole that might get wider as I walked along. I'd be hard put to it to get any more if they did, because I hadn't got a penny to my name. Admitted, I could always stop and ask people to give me a match, but it was risky, because I'd often tried it, though sometimes I managed to beg one or two from a bloke who didn't care what I was up to and perhaps wanted me to smoke myself to death, or set Nottingham on fire. But mostly the people I asked either pushed me away and said clear off, or told me they were sorry but their matches were safeties and no good without a box. Now and again a bloke with safeties would give me a few anyway—wanting to help me and hoping I'd find some way to strike them, though I never did, unless I lit them with proper matches I latched on to later. The people I never asked were women, after the first one or two had threatened to fetch a copper, being clever enough to twig what I was up to.

Wind blew my hair about as I crossed the railway bridge by the station. Trolley buses trundled both ways and mostly empty, though even if I'd had a penny I'd still have walked, for walking my legs off made me feel I was going somewhere, strolling along though not too slow and enjoying the faces of fresh air that met me by the time I got out to the open spaces of Western Boulevard. I was feeling free and easy, and hoped a copper wouldn't stop me and ask what I was doing with paper and matches sticking out of my pockets. But nobody bothered me and I turned down from the bridge and onto the canal bank, looking in deep locks now and again, at the endless bottoms of water, as if the steep sides of the smooth wall still went on underneath—to the middle of the earth as far as I knew. A funny thought came to me: how long would it take for this canyon with water at the bottom to be filled to the brim with the fine and flimsy ash from cigarettes, only that? I sat on a lock gate and wondered: how many people need to smoke how many fags for how many years? Donkey's years, I supposed. I'd be an old man on two sticks by then. Even teachers at school wouldn't be able to work that sum out. I stood up and had a long pee down into the smooth surface, my pasty face in the mirror of it shivered to bits when the first piss struck.

After a good while of more walking I cut off along a lane at the next bridge leading towards the wood I'd set my heart on: a toy for Christmas. I was excited, already heard fire-engines crossing the sky, bells going off miles away, a sound that thrilled me even though I did know I was hearing things. The wheat was tall, yellow and dusty-looking over hedges and gates, bushes so high along the lane that sometimes I couldn't see the sky. Faded fag packets and scorched newspaper had been thrown among nettles and scrub by lads and courting couples out from Nottingham, for the fields weren't all that far off from the black and smothercating streets. My teeth still felt funny at the screams of tree-trunks from Sunday overtime at the sawmill not far off, though after a while I couldn't hear anything at all, except the odd thrush or blackbird nipping about like bats trying to get their own shadows in their beaks. I'd been out here a time or two with pals looking for eggs in birds' nests but I wasn't interested in that any more because my uncle once caught me with some and told me it was wicked and wrong to rob birds of their young 'uns.

So I walked by the hedge, keeping well down till I got to a gap. It was dim and cool in the wood, and so lonely that I'd have been frightened if I hadn't a pocketful of paper and matches to keep me company. Bushes were covered in blackberries, and I stopped now and again to take my pick, careful not to scratch myself or eat too many in case I got the gut ache when I went to bed at night.

It was long and narrow, not the sort of wood you could go deep into, so I jumped over a stream and found the middle quick enough, a clearing, more or less, with a dry and dying bush on one side that looked just ready for a fire. I worked like a galley slave, piling up dead twigs and leaves over my bit of paper that soon you could hardly see. I wondered about the noise but what could I do? and anyway soon forgot my worry and went on working. I knew it must be past dinner-time when I stood back to look at my bonfire heap. Sweating like a bull (though nothing to how them trees would be sweating in a bit, I grinned) I measured the chances of a fire-engine fire: the bush was sure to light and so would the two small trees on either side, but unless there was a good wind the main trees would be hard put to it.

The first match was slammed out by the wind that blew strong over my shoulder as if it had been lurking there specially; the head of the second fell off before I could get under the paper; the third-time lucky one caught a treat, was like a red, red robin breaking out of its shell, and I soon had to stand back to keep the burning blazes off my hand. I wanted to put it out at first: the words nearly choked me: 'Stread on it. Kick it to bits.' I twisted my hands up in front of me, but couldn't move, just stood there like the no good tripehound dad often called me (and which I dare say I was) until the smoke made me step further back—and back I went until my head scraped into a big-barked tree. The noise of the fire must have been what frightened me: it was as hungry as if it had got teeth, went chewing its way up into the air like a shark in Technicolor. A stone of blood settled over my heart, but smoke and flame hypnotized me, stood me there frozen and happy, rubbing my hands yet wanting to put it out, but not being able to any more than I could kill myself.

I didn't know fires could grow like that. My little ones had always gone out, shrunk up to black bits and flew into the air when I set half a breath against it. But then, that was only true with a scrap of newspaper on an asphalt yard. This was in a wood, and fire took to it like a kid to hot dinners: it was a sheet of red flame and grey smoke, a choking wall and curtain that scared me a bit, because I was back to life, as if big hands would reach out and grab me in for good and all. Like my uncle had said hell was—though I never believed him till now.

It was time to run. I sped off like a rabbit, scratched and cindered as my ankles caught on thorns and sharp grass. The hammer-and-tongs of a fire-engine were a long way from me now, and I was a ragged-arsed thunderbolt suddenly tangled in a high bush, stuck like a press-stud that fought a path out, and went on again lit-up and cursing. At the edge of the wood I slowed down, and half-way to the lane looked back, expecting to see a sheet of fire and smoke bending out over the trees with flags flying and claws sharp.

But nothing. I could have burst into a gallon of tears. Nothing: not a butterfly of smoke, not an ant of flame. Maybe I'm too close to see, I thought. Or should I run back and stoke up again, blow it and coax, pat and kick it into life? But I went on. If the wood caught fire, as I still hoped, who'd get the fire-engines? And if nobody did would I hear and see them? Being as how I'd caused the fire I had to get miles away quick without being spotted, so how could I poke my nose in at the nearest copperbox and bawl out there was a fire in Snakey Wood and not risk getting sent to an Approved School for my good deed? I wished I'd thought of this already, but all I could hope for now was that some bloke at the local sawmill or a field-digger from the farm would twig things while I wasn't too far off and get the fire-engine on its way so's I could run and see it.

By the lane I turned, and there it was: no fire yet but a thin trail of smoke coming up like a wavy blue pole above the crowded trees. I'd expected it all to be like it was on the pictures, boiling away and me having to run for my life, with a yellow-orange carpet of flame snap-dragging at my heels, but it just showed how different things were to what you expected. Not that I didn't know they always were, but it still came as a shock I don't mind admitting. The wood was burning, which was a start, and though I couldn't see any flame yet I didn't wait for it either, but dodged under the hedgebottom and crossed the open field to the big outstanding arm-beam of a canal lock. I puffed and grunted to get it shut, then crept across on all fours—using it as a bridge—to the towing path on the other side. Nobody saw me: a man was humped over the bank fishing a bit further down, but he never even turned to see who was passing. Maybe he ain't got a licence to fish, I thought, and no more wants to be seen than I do—which I can easy understand.

The wind blew stronger and the sun still shone but I daren't look back towards my pet wood which I hoped by now was crackling away to boggery. Walking along I looked like a fed-up kid out for an airing who was too daft and useless to have been in mischief—but because it seemed as if butter wouldn't melt in my mouth didn't mean I hadn't set a fire off in which butter wouldn't stand an earthly. I didn't want anybody to twig anything though, as I walked up to the main road and into a world of people and traffic where I wasn't so noticeable any more.

Back along the canal, far-off thick smoke was going up to the bubble-blue sky, black low down as if from an oil-well, but thinning a bit on top. It was burning all right, though people walking by didn't seem to think much was amiss. I sat on the bridge wall, unable to take my eyes off it, rattled a bit that people didn't turn to open their mouths and wonder what I was looking at. I wanted to shout out: 'Hey missis, hey mester, see that smoke? It's Snakey Wood on fire, and I done it'—but somehow the words wouldn't come, though God knows I remember wanting them to.

I started off towards home, one minute happy that I'd brought off my own big fire, and the next crippled by a rotten sadness I couldn't explain, hands in pockets as I walked further and further away from the column of my fire and smoke that, if you think about it, should have made me the happiest kid in Radford.

From this changeable mood I was neither one thing nor the other as I went downhill towards the White Horse—almost home—having nothing else in my head but a shrill-whistled Al Jolson tune. Then into my ears and brain—through the last barbed-wire of my whistling—came the magic sound I'd longed all day to hear. The air went blue and electric, as it sometimes does before a terrible sheet-ripping thunderstorm, and cars at the crossroads stopped and waited, drivers winding their windows down to look out. My mouth opened and I stared and stared, the only picture in my mind for the next few seconds being that of the last bonfire night but one, in which I'd wandered off on my own up Mitchell Street and come across the best fire I'd ever seen. It was already twice as high as any man, and impossible to stoke anything else on top. A pile of mattresses still had got to be burned and a couple of big lads dragged them one at a time up on top of a chapel roof by whose side-walls the fire had been lit. When all of the two dozen bug-eaten mattresses were stacked high on the slates, the lads swung each one out, perched up there like demons in the blaze of the rattling flames, and let them crash down one by one into the very middle of the red bed. Everybody said the church would go, but it didn't, and when I saw that it wouldn't I walked away.

My eyes were open again on broad daylight, and from the

top of the opposite hill sounded the bells I remembered hearing that very first time as a kid when downtown with mam. But this time there were more bells than I'd ever heard; a big red engine, fresh out of the vast sheds of town and coming between the shops and pubs, shot the crossroads as if out of a flashgun, all bells at full throttle so that two blokes talking outside the pub couldn't make themselves heard and stopped till it had gone by. But they still couldn't start talking again, because another engine was almost right behind.

My legs trembled and I thought my ears would fall away from my head. One of the two men looked so hard at me that his face swam, and I thought: What's he making himself go all blurred like that for?—but when my ankles became heavy as lead and my legs above them turned into feathers I knew it was my eyes swimming, that I was about to cave in again like I'd done that long time ago with mam. I took a step forward, screwing my eyes and opening them, then held on the window ledge for a second, until I knew I'd be all right, and was able to stand another engine bursting in and out of my brain; then another.

Four! No sooner could I have shouted with joy, than I found it hard to stop myself letting the tears roll like wagons out of my eyes. I'd never seen four fire-engines before. The whole wood must be in flame from top to bottom, I thought, and was sorry now I hadn't stayed close by to watch, wondering if I should go back, because I knew that even four engines wouldn't get a fire like that down before tonight or even later. All that work and walking gone for nothing, I cursed, as another engine broke the record of the last one down the hill. I waved as it shot by, yet felt as if I'd had my fill of fire-engines for a long while.

Six passed altogether. By this time I was sobbing, almost stone-dead and useless. 'What's up, kid?' one of the two men said to me.

'I'm frightened,' I managed to blurt out. He patted me on the shoulder. 'There's no need o' that. The fire's miles away, up Wollaton somewhere, by the look on it. It wain't come down 'ere, so you needn't worry.' But I couldn't stop. It was as hard to dry up as it had been for me to start, and I went on heaving as if the end of the world was just around the corner.

'Do you live far?' he asked.

'I'm frightened,' was all I said, and he didn't know what to do, wished by this time he'd left me alone: 'Well, you shouldn't be frightened. You're a big lad now.'

I walked towards home along Eddison Road, my eyes drying up with every step, the great stone in my chest not jumping about so much. Six fire-engines made it a bigger day than Christmas, each red engine being better than a Santa Claus, so that even after my firebugging I never got over red being my favourite colour. When I went in through the scullery dad looked happy, and such a thing was hard for me to understand.

'Come on my old lad,' he said. I'd never seen him so good-tempered. 'Where've you bin all this time, you young bogger? It's nearly tea time.' He pulled a chair to the table for me: 'Here you are, get this down you. You must be clambed to death'—took a plate of dinner out of the oven. 'I thought you'd got lost, or summat. Your mam's bin asking for you.'

'Is she all right then, dad?'

'She's a bit better today,' he smiled. 'I expect we'll pull her through yet'—which I was so glad to hear that it made me twice as hungry, as if the fire had burned a hole in me as well as Snakey Wood, because a whole load of food was needed to fill it. Dad brought in the teapot, and I drank two mugs of that as well. 'My Christ,' he said, sitting opposite me with a fag on and enjoying the sight of me eating, 'I heard a lot of fire-engines going by just now. Some poor bogger's getting burned out of house and home by the sound of it.'

Nobody knew who started that big fire all them years ago, and I know now that nobody will ever care, because Snakey Wood has gone forever, even better flattened than by any fire. Its trees have been ripped up and soil pressed down by a housing estate that spread over it. As it turned out I only burned down half, according to the *Post*, and though everybody in our yard knew I was a bit of a firebug nobody thought for a minute it might have been me who set fire to Snakey Wood. Or if they did, nowt was said.

In the next load of weeks and months I lost all interest in lighting fires. Even the sound of a fire-engine rattling by didn't bother me as much as it had. Maybe it was strange, me giving it up all of a sudden like that, but I just hadn't got the heart to put match to paper, couldn't be bothered in fact, after mam got better—which happened about the same time. I expect that big fire satisfied me, because whatever I did again would need to be bloody huge to get more than six engines called out to it. In any case there was something bigger than me to start fires, for after a couple of years came an air raid from the Germans and I remember getting out of the shelter at six one morning when the all-clear had gone and standing in the middle of our street, seeing the whole sky red and orange over the other side of Nottingham—where, I heard later, two whole factories were up in flames. They burned for days, and I wanted to go off and see them but dad wouldn't let me. People said that fifty fire-engines had to come before that was put out—spinning into Nottingham from Mansfield and Derby and all over everywhere.

And not long afterwards I was fourteen, went to work and started courting, so what was the use of fires after that?

THE MAGIC BOX

I

Fred made his way towards the arboretum bench.

Though it was well gone eleven he hadn't yet clocked in, and wouldn't, either. There were some things a man would be glad to work for, but that morning his head was full of thoughts that would have got him hung—if anything could have been gained by swinging.

He sat down, drew two porkpies from their cellophane wrappers and exposed them to daylight. Half closing his eyes (as if his palate were up there and not in his mouth) he bit into the first pie: the meat wasn't bad, but the pastry was chronic. When the crumpled bag settled in the prison of the half-filled litter basket he chewed through a prolonged stare towards the ornamental pond and park wall, hearing the breathtaking gear-change of traffic chewing its way up the hill outside.

Morning was the worse time. He hated going to bed, and he hated getting up even more, but since these two actions were necessary for life and work he preferred getting up—by himself. God alone knew why Nan had risen with him this morning, but she had, and that, as much as anything else, had been the cause of the row that had burst over them—from her. In six years of marriage he'd learned that to argue at breakfast always led to a blow-up. It was better to argue in the evening (if you had any choice) because sooner or later you went to bed.

Though in many ways pleasant, half a day off work wasn't the sort of thing he could keep from Nan, since she saw his wage packet on Friday night. Not that she nosed into every-thing, but her skill at housekeeping demanded that each bob and tanner be accounted for. He would be laughed at by his workmates if they knew, though many of them lived by the same arrangement, and that was a fact. In any case how could they find out? Nan wouldn't drive by in a speaker van and let them know, for she often claimed: 'My place is to go shopping and clean the house, not to wait for you outside that stinking factory. When we go to the pictures on Friday you can get me a place in the queue, and I'll meet you there.'

He only hoped that one day Nan would see him as the good man from the many bad, a bloke who didn't deserve to be bossed and tormented so much. But she hated the factory, as if to punish him not only for having married her but also for stipulating soon after that she should stop going out to work. He'd only insisted on it because he loved her, thinking she wanted him to press her on this and prove even greater love than he was capable of. Not many would have loved a woman enough to see it that way. But since the gilt had worn off she became bitter about having left work at all, hinting that staying on would have made her a forewoman by now. In fact she had only offered to give in to his manly insistence because she wanted him to see that she loved him more than was considered normal, and he had been blind and selfish enough to take her up on it.

'Well'—now wanting some peace in the house—'why don't you go and ask them to set you on again if that's the way you feel? I'm not a bleddy mind reader.'

This took the row to a higher pitch, as he'd known it would, but he hadn't the sense to sit down and say nothing, or walk out of the house whistling. 'How can I?' she called. 'I'd have to start again on a machine. I'd never get back to the old position I had when I was loony enough to take note o' you and pack my good job in.'

He didn't know how it had begun that morning. He didn't suppose she did, either. He would like to think of her as still brooding on it, but not likely. No sooner had the door closed than she'd smashed the cup he'd drunk from, though he'd bet his last dollar she was out shopping now, and laughing with other women as if there'd been no quarrel at all.

It was fine enough weather to make everyone forget their troubles. Autumn sun warmed the green banks of the park, ants and insects proliferating among juicy-looking blades of grass. Small birds fed at a piece of his cast-off porkpie beyond the diamond wirespaces of the litter basket, like a dozen thumbnail sketches that had come to life. Two pigeons joined the feast, enormous in comparison to the thrushes, but there was no bullying. Both pigeons and thrushes seemed unaware of any difference in size, and the fact that both wanted to get at the same piece of pie was, after all, a similarity.

He smoked a cigarette. A young man walked by with a back-combed suicide-blonde in a black mac, who looked as if she hadn't had a square meal for a month, and she was saying angrily: 'I'll bleddy-well nail him when I see him, I bleddy-well will, an' all'—with such threat and vengeance that Fred felt sorry for whoever this was meant. The world thrives on it, he thought, but I don't, and in any case life's not always like that. Bad luck and good luck: it's like a swing on a kids playground, always one thing or the other. We've had more than our share of the bad though, by bloody Christ we have, too much to think about, and the last bit of good luck was almost more trouble than it was worth. He thought back on it, how a year ago, at the start of the football season, a cheque had come one morning for two hundred and fifty quid, and a few hours later his mug (and Nan's) was grinning all over the front of the newspaper. She enjoyed it so much that it certainly didn't occur to him to remind her of all the times she had threatened to burn the daft football coupons on which he had wasted so much time and money. No, they got in a dozen quarts of beer and a platter of black puddings, and handed manna around to anyone with the grace or avarice to drop in. The man from the *Post* had asked: 'What are you going to do with the money?' Fred was surprised at so much bother when all he felt was disappointment at not hitting the treble chance and raking in a hundred thousand. Two hundred and fifty nicker seemed so little that before Nan could spin some tale or intent to the reporter Fred butted in: 'Oh, I expect we'll just split it and use it as pocket-money.' Which was duly noted in heavy type for the day's editions (POOLS WIN: POCKET-MONEY FOR NOTTINGHAM COUPLE) so prominently displayed that though Nan had the spirit left to tell Fred he should have kept his trap shut she hadn't the nerve to make him do anything else with the money but what he'd said he would for fear of being known to defy the bold public print of a newspaper that, as far as Nan knew, everyone had read.

To spend a hundred quid in one fell bout of shopping demanded bravery, and Fred was the sort in which, if bravery existed, it was anything but spontaneous. Still, he had seen things worth buying which, so far, was more than could be said for Nan. Walking around town Fred had come across an all-wave ex-army wireless receiver staring him out from behind plate glass, the exact communications set he'd worked during his war stint with the signals in Egypt. It stayed in the same window for months, being, he surmised, too expensive for anyone to step in and say: 'I want it.' So he took his time in sparking up courage to walk by that array of valves and morse tappers, to make a purchase by pointing between heart beats towards the window.

Many afternoons he'd stood at the window fixed by the magic black box of the communications receiver, and at so many long and regular absences Nan began to wonder whether he had set himself up with a piece of fancy work met in the factory—and she said as much when he once came home looking piqued and sheepish. He still hadn't been able to walk in and buy the radio, and so felt poor enough in spirit to go straight over and kiss her: 'Hello, my angel, how are we today?'

She turned her face away. Half a dozen books were stacked on the sideboard after a visit to the library. 'What's the idea? What do you want?'

'I don't want anything.'

'You'd better not, either, until you tell me where you go and what you get up to every Saturday afternoon.'

So that was what he'd seen boiling up, something so far from his mind that he could only say: 'I've bin down town looking around the shops.'

She pulled the curtains across and set the table, while Fred dug himself in the fireside chair, watching her as she worked. Her face had altered, become sterner in the last year or two, as if it had done enough battle with the world since Ivor had been drowned. But at thirty she was still good-looking, pretty almost, with her small even features and smooth skin. Her face was round and pleasantly fleshed, her eyes cool and outgiving when she was not anguished or perturbed. He smiled as she reached into the crockery cupboard: the best might be yet to come. How can she think I'd ever look at another woman? We've been through a lot together, the worst of it being the terrible way that Ivor went. If there's anything worse than her blaming me for him having fallen into that canal while reaching for a batch of tadpoles, it's her blaming herself, which I know she does even though it was three years ago and an accident. To think we paid that batchy girl half a crown every time she took him out, and she let this happen. My first thought on hearing he'd been killed like that was: 'The daft little bogger. Wait till I get my hands on him. I'll give him what for.' I couldn't believe it then, but I can now, just about.

'Have you been looking at the shops thinking how to spend your football money?' she asked in a more amiable voice, passing a cup of tea. They'd married on his demob leave in forty-six, after a mere week of kisses five years before, and four hundred letters in which by an inexhaustable permutation every aspect of common romantic love had been exchanged between them. Distance had made both hearts grow fonder, and out of sight out of mind had been disproved, apart from the long letters, by a frequent transmission of photographic images on which were stamped the thousand proofs of far-off love that kept Fred and Nan alive for each other. It was as if they were married after the first three months apart, as if they had already spent a honeymoon at Matlock and been wrenched from it by the first year, and had been long settled into an unthinking matrimonial rut by the fourth. They wrote of houses and work and children, and by the time they stood outside the church posing for their first photo together Fred anyway felt that the marriage about to begin was a plain print of black and white on positive paper, as opposed to the flimsy and transient negative of the preceding years.

Nan didn't see it like this, found it necessary to distinguish between the correspondence course and her new full status as a housewife, became more competent than Fred at tackling problems after returning from a week at Matlock. To go shopping—pale, young and full of thought—in the raw fog of a December morning and come home to see that the fire had died, brought reality closer than Fred's daily dash to his factory incarceration in which machines warmly hummed and men baited him still on his recent honeymoon. Through the war Nan had stayed in a cold and exacting climate, while Fred had picked dreamily at radio sets in his monastic army life. Fascinated by the Nile Valley, he had ventured with his pals on a trip to the Great Pyramid, and his lean young unsure face looked down from the high back of a camel in a Box Brownie snapshot sent to Nan who, though stuck with the hardships of air-raids and rationing, saw him as adventuring around wild desert with an independence boding good for when they were married.

Not that she'd had much to complain about; in fact during her pregnancy Fred was as good as gold—she told her mother. And when Ivor came along he was even better, so she was now in the position of knowing that something was wrong yet not being able to complain, a state for which she couldn't but blame him, and which led to frenzied unreasonable quarrels which he could only define as 'temper' and blame on her.

'You're always curious about how I'm going to spend my share of the football money,' he said, 'but you haven't got rid of your whack yet. What are you going to do with it?' Answers to this question lacked venom, for money was now the only discussable topic which did not disturb the unstable bed of their emotions. She looked up from the newspaper: 'I haven't thought about it much, though I daresay I shall one of these days.'

A waterhen went out from the nearest bank, going as smoothly over the water as if drawn by a piece of cotton pulled by an invisible boy on the other side. Its head with button-eye and yellow beak was perfectly proud and still, and the green and blue back-feathers were comparable to colours made by flames appearing on the surface of a fire that had acted dead and out. The sun was good, and he didn't intend going to work until after dinner-hour, even if it meant another big row with Nan. The sound of machinery would cripple all reflection, and its manufacturing teeth pulling him back like a bulldog to earning a living for himself, Nan, and a possible future kid, seemed appalling in this unexpected sunshine—just as did the idea of going home to Nan again after their awful purposeless scrap of the morning.

It was the first time such a thing had happened, and it gnawed at his peace of mind because he'd had no intention of pushing her back so hard against the sofa. His hand had left the hot side of the cup and collided with her before he could do anything about it. It frightened him. If only I'd done it deliberately, known what was in me. The gone-out stare in her face drove him from the house, and he doubted whether he'd get back into it. Then again maybe she'd have forgotten it by evening, which would only go to show how much effect these rows had on her. He wasn't even sure he wanted to get back into the house anyway. Out of it the pain was less, and sitting in the park having eaten two pork pies and a thimble of sunshine sent it right away except for occasional stabs of the memory knife.

He walked through the main gate, towards the radio shop in the middle thoroughfare of the driving city. His football winnings took on value at last, a lump sum of over a hundred pounds to be handed in for a high-class radio set that would put him in touch with the short-wave world, give something to do and maybe stop him being such a bastard to Nan. If he ordered it now the shop van would deliver it tomorrow. And after the dinner-hour he'd go back to work, otherwise, with it being Friday, he would get no wages.

II

Earphones on, he sat alone in Ivor's room, tuned-in to the Third Programme like a resistance radio operator receiving from abroad instructions that were the life blood of his cause.

A fastidious voice was speaking unintelligibly on books and, as if not getting his money's worth, Fred clicked on to short wave and sent the needle rippling over hundreds of morse stations. Sounds chipped and whistled like clouds of tormented birds trying to get free, but he fixed one station and, as if from the fluttering of wings pinned firm at the middle by the hair-thin tuning needle, he deciphered its rhythm as: MEET ME TILBURY DOCK THURSDAY 24TH STOP AM DYING TO BE WITH YOU AGAIN ALL MY LOVE DARLING—MARY.

Alistair Crossbanks, 3 Hearthrug Villas, Branley was the lucky man, yet not the only one, since Fred took several more such messages. They came from sea-liners and went to waiting lovers who burned with the anguish of tormented separation —though he doubted whether any had spanned the same long time as Nan and himself before they were married. But the thought of ships steaming through a broadly striped sea at its sudden tropical darkening caused him to ignore further telegrams. He pictured a sleek liner in a thousand miles of ocean, a great circle bordering its allotted speed as, day after day, it crawled on an invisible track towards Aden or Capetown. He felt its radio pulse beating softly in his ear, as if by listening he had some control of it, and the remoteness of this oceanic lit-up beetle set off his own feeling of isolation in this sea-like suburb spreading in terraces and streets around his room.

The room had belonged to Ivor before he had been killed. Wallpaper of rabbits and trees, trains and aeroplanes, suggested it, as well as the single bed and the cupboard of toys that, even so long afterwards, neither had the heart to empty. Ivor had dark hair and brown eyes, and up to the age of four had been sharp and intelligent, thin, voracious and bright, all running and fighting, wanting and destroying. Yet for several months before slipping into the cold pocket of the canal he had turned back from this unnatural liveliness as if, not having such life responded to, the world had failed to get through to him, to make touch with his spirit in a way he could understand. Fred couldn't even regret having ill-treated him—that anyway would have made him easier remembered. All he saw was his wild boy breaking up an alarm clock and screaming off into a corner when the bell jangled his unready ears. But the lasting image of Ivor's face was one of deprivation, and this was what Fred could not explain, for it wasn't lack of food, clothes, toys, even money that gave this peculiar look, but an expression—now he saw it clearly—bound into Ivor's soul, one that would never let him respond to them.

He threw the master switch, and sat in evening silence, overpowered by this bleak force of negative feedback. Trust me to blame an innocent dead kid for what could only have been my fault and maybe Nan's. Ships were moving over untroubled oceans, set in such emptiness and warmth that for the people on them the tree of ecstasy was still a real thing. He switched on and, by the hairsplitting mechanism of the magic box, such poems were extractable out of the atmosphere. Another telegram from ELIZABETH said HOPE YOU BOOKED US A ROOM STOP CAN'T WAIT, and to break such torment he turned to news agency Tass explaining some revolutionary method of oil drilling in the Caucasus—a liquid cold chute of morse that cleared all passion from his mind.

He stayed undisturbed in Ivor's room, knowing that Nan would sit feasting at the television until calling him down for supper at half-past nine. He felt strange tonight; a bad tormenting cold depressed him: at such times his senses were connected to similar bad colds in the past, and certain unwrapped scenes from them hit him with stunning vividness.

Egypt was a land of colds, brought on by a yearly inundation of the Nile widening its valley into a sea of water and mud. Triangular points of the dark brown pyramids that reared beyond appeared sordid, like old jettisoned cartons fallen somehow in such queer shape, and looking from this distance as if, should a prolonged breeze dry them of rain and flood-water, a more violent wind might uproot and lose them in the open desert like so much rubbish. In Cairo he had been a champion at morse, writing it at thirty-two words a minute and reading it at thirty-six. His brain, perfect for reception, drew in streams of morse for hour after hour and jerked his fingers to rapid script with no thought barrier between, work from which other less dedicated operators were led glassy-eyed and muttering to some recuperation camp by the blistering bonny banks of the Suez Canal. Fred enjoyed his fame as speed king, which, though pre-supposing a certain yoga-like emptiness of mind, demanded at the same time a smart brain and a dab hand. Yet in nothing did he look speedy: his sallow face made him seem always deep in slow thoughts beyond the understanding of his noisier pals—who were less efficient as radio men. Their respect for him was for his seriousness as much as for an uncommon rate of morse, which must have been so because even those in the cookhouse, to whom signalling prowess meant nothing, didn't bawl so sharply when a gap lay between Fred and the plate-filling man ahead. He was a priest of silence among blades of bed-tipping and boozing, singing and bawling and brothel-going. Some who didn't muck-in were subjected at least to apple-pie beds, but Fred was on good terms even without trying. He was somehow found congenial, and would often have tea brought back for him from the mess by someone who came off watch at a late hour. When Fred returned this favour it was even more appreciated for being unexpected.

Mostly he would sit by himself in the library writing long letters to Nan, but the one friend he made was flown up one day from Kenya in the belly of a Mosquito fighter-bomber—which dropped its extra fuel tanks like turds somewhere over the desert. The shortage of good operators was so desperate (at a time of big offensive or retreat—nobody could ever tell which, since all differences were drowned in similar confusion) that Fred was working a hundred hours a week. Not that he felt shagged by it, but the Big Battle had started and another man was needed, so in stepped Peter Nkagwe, a tall cheek-scarred black African from Nairobi—freshly changed into clean pressed khaki drill and smiling a good afternoon boys as he entered the signals office. The sergeant assigned him a set, and Fred amazed, then envious, saw his long-fingered hands trembling the key like a concert pianist at an evenness and speed never before seen.

Peter Nkagwe was no ascetic sender and receiver like Fred,

but smiled and looked around as he played the key with an accurate, easy, show-off proficiency. He not only read Reuter's cricket scores from Australia but, which was where Fred failed, his fingers were nimble enough to write them down, so that his sheets of neat script went from hand to hand around the base until falling apart.

One day Fred called over, words unrehearsed, ignited from such depth that he didn't even regret them after he'd spoken: 'You beat out them messages, mate, like you was at a tom-tom.'

Peter, unflinching, finished the message at his usual speed. He then took off his earphones and stood over Fred in silence.

Fred was uncomfortable at the length of it: 'Lost owt?'

'There's a look in your eyes, MATE,' Peter said, 'as if your head's full of shit.' He went back to his radio, and from then on Fred's signalling championship was divided. They became friends.

Night after night at his communications receiver, Fred hoped to hear messages from his old HQ unit that, though long closed down, would magically send the same signals rippling between familiar stations. He might even pick up the fast melodious rhythms of Peter Nkagwe, that vanished ghost of a friend who, somewhere, still sat keying out indispensable messages whose text and meaning, put into code and cypher by someone else, was never made known to him. He turned the dial slowly, hoping to recognize both callsign and sending prowess of his old friend. It was impossible, though much time at the set was spent shamefaced in this way as if, should he try hard and stay at it long enough, those lost voices would send out tentacles and pull him back to the brilliant sun-dazzle of the Mokattam Hills.

His lean face, and expert hands moving over the writing-pad, were set before his multi-dialled altar, the whole outlined by a tassel-shaded table lamp. If I'd had this radio in Ivor's day, he laughed, the little bogger would have been at it till the light didn't shine and the valves packed in. Talk about destruction! 'Destruction, thy name is Ivor!' He remembered him, as if he were downstairs drinking tea, or being bathed in front of the fire, or gone away to his grandma's and due back next week. Anything mechanical he'd smash. He took a day on a systematic wipe-out of the gramophone, then brought the pieces to Fred, who suggested he put them together again. Ivor tried (I will say that for him) but failed, and when Fred mended it he was so overjoyed at the record spinning loud and true once more that he treated it as one thing to stay henceforth free of his hammer.

Ivor with a round, empty-eyed happiness, took huge bites of bread, and wiped jamstains down his shirt. Fred couldn't keep the sarcasm from his voice when telling him to stop, so that the bites had changed to tiny, until Fred laughed and they returned to big again, relaxing the empty desperation of his tough face. Such memories were buried deep, going down like the different seams and galleries of a coalmine. In the few months before his birth Ivor had moved inside Nan, kicking with life that had been distinct enough to wake Fred at night— and send him back to sleep smiling.

The small lamp gave one-tenth light, leaving most of the room in darkness. Fixed at the muttering radio and reaping an occasional message out of the air with his fast-moving hook of a pencil, Fred felt his mind locked in the same ratio, with that one tenth glimmer unable to burst like a bomb and explode the rest of himself into light. He composed silent questions about Ivor, like sending out telegrams that would get no answer. Why was I born? Why didn't I love him so that he stayed alive? Could I love anybody enough to make them stay alive and kicking? Would it have made any difference if I'd loved him even more than I did? He couldn't lift the dominating blackness from his brain, but struggled to free himself, ineffectually spinning the knobs and dials of his radio, fighting to keep even the one-tenth light in his consciousness.

He opened the radio lid and peered in at the valves, coloured lights of blue flame deep in bulbs as if he had cultivated in his one-tenth light a new shape of exotic onion. Thoughts passed through his mind, singly and in good order, though the one just gone was never remembered—only the sensation remained that it had been. He tried to recall the thought or picture slipping from his mind in order to lynchpin it to the one now pushing in—which might, he hoped, be seen to have some connection to the one following. It turned out to have nothing in common at all.

'Never mind, sweetheart,' I said, when Ivor was drowned. 'Never mind'—rocking her back to sense. But she turned on him, words burning now as if he had taken them down in morse: 'Always "My sweetheart",' she cried. 'You never say "My wife".' He was hurt and bitter, unable to understand, but saw now that not saying 'My wife' and never getting through to Ivor with his love, were the same thing.

The earphones blocked all sounds of children, traffic, next-door telly, and he wrote another message from the spot-middle of some ocean or other, a man-made arrowhead of peace steering from land to land: ARRIVING HOME 27TH CAN'T WAIT TO SEE MY MUMMY AND DADDY—LOVE JANET. The big ship sailed on: aerials sensitive, funnels powerful, people happy—sleeping, eating, kissing or, if crew, heavy with work. He saw himself in a smaller craft, marooned in a darkening unmapped ocean where no one sent messages because he was the only passenger, and no person would think to flash him a telegram anyway. Neither could anyone wish him a good journey because he had never announced his port of destination, and in any case no one knew he was afloat, and there was no one to whom he could send a marconi-gram stating his imminent arrival because even if he were going somewhere he wouldn't even know where nor when he would get there, and there was even less chance of anyone being at that end than from where he'd started. All he could do was fight this vision, and instead keep the big jewel-lit liner in his mind, read what messages flashed to and from it.

Earphones swung from the jacks-socket, and in the full overhead light he snapped open Ivor's cupboard. Horses and trainsets, teddybear and games and forts and tricycle were piled where the boy had last thrown them. Morse sounds no longer hit him like snowflakes from his lit-up fabulous ship. He stared blindly as each toy was slung across the room, towards window, door, fireplace or ceiling, until every limbless piece had found a new resting place. He went back to his wireless as the stairfoot door snapped open and heavy sounds thumped their way up at his commotion.

The ship remained. Its messages of love and arrival for some, godspeed for others, birthday wishes and the balming oil of common news, still sped out from it; but such words from the black box made a picture that he couldn't break like the limbless toys all around him. His breath scraped out of his lungs at the real and coloured vision mercilessly forming. The ship was off centre, but he was able to watch it slowly sinking, the calm grey water of tropical dusk lapping around it with cat-like hunger, as if finely controlled by a brain not apparent or visible to anyone. The ship subsided to its decks, and the endless oil-smooth sea became more easy-going and polite, though kept the hidden strength to force it under. As the ship flooded, people overflowed the lifeboats, until nothing remained but an undisturbed grey sheet of water—as smooth and shiny as tin that can be used for a mirror—and a voice in the earphones saying something Fred could not at first decipher. It was a gruff, homely, almost familiar tone, though one that he knew he would never be able to recognize no matter how long he concentrated.

The lock on the bedroom door burst, and several people were trying to pull him away from the radio, Nan's voice imploring above the others. Fingers of both hands—white and strong as flayed twigs—held on to the radio, which was so heavy that those pulling at him thought it was nailed to the bench and that the bench was rivetted to the floor. Fred held on with great strength, without speaking, cunning enough at the crucial moment to withdraw his hands from the radio (before superior odds could pull him clear) and clamp them with an equally steel-grip on to the bench, strange grunts sounding like trapped animals trying to jump from his mouth.

Eventually they dragged him free. Sweat glistened on him, as he waved his arms in the middle of the room: 'I heard God!' he shouted. 'Leave me be,' he roared. 'I heard God!'— then dropped.

III

Nan said not to bother with a doctor and, when they argued, stood to her full height, thanked everyone very much, and bundled them out of the house. Neighbours were a godsend, but there was an end to what goodness you could let them show. When Fred was undressed and into bed she stood by the window of Ivor's room, wondering why exactly he'd had such a fit. Hadn't he been happy? As far as she knew he lacked nothing, had all that most men had. She thought a lot of him, in spite of everything, and was quite sure he thought a lot of her, in spite of the fact that he was incapable of showing it. Neither had any reproaches to make, and apart from poor Ivor being drowned their life hadn't been so bad. Of course, she could never understand how he'd survived Ivor's death so well, though maybe it was bravery and self control that hadn't let him show what this barbaric piece of luck had done to him—which was all very well, but such dumb silence had made it ten times worse for her. She'd paid for it, by God, and it had just about done her in. It was hard to believe he'd felt it as hard as she had, in any case, when the first action of his fit had been to pulverise poor Ivor's toys. That wasn't something she could forgive and forget in a hurry, even though he may not have realized what he was doing. If he'd been full of drink it would have been a different matter, maybe, but Fred only drank much at Christmas or birthdays. Still, it wasn't like him to have such a black paralytic fit.

Next morning she phoned a doctor. He was violent and screaming all night, had ripped off great strips of wallpaper in his unreachable agony. During these long hours she was reminded of a new-born baby gripped for no reason by a blind unending temper, and there is nothing to do except draw on all the patience you have and try to soothe. Thinking of this kept her calm and able to manage. In a few bleak minutes of early morning she persuaded him to enter a mental hospital. 'I don't want you to go, love. But everybody thinks it'll be for the best. And I think so as well. They know what to do about such things there. You'll be as right as rain then in a couple of months.'

'All right,' he said, unable to care. Afloat in the ocean like his favourite unanchorable ship, he was carried away by a restful warm current beyond anyone's control.

She packed a case as if he were going again on a five-year jag to the army. She looked anxious and sorry, unable to stop her tears falling, her hand trembling as she turned out drawers for handkerchiefs and pyjamas. Fred sat in the arm-chair, his dressing-gown collar pulled up to his white immobile face, shaking with cold though the room was warmed by a huge, expert fire.

She travelled in the ambulance and saw him into the hospital, registered, examined, sedated, finally laid full-length in a narrow immaculate bed. Everything happened so quickly that she began to doubt that they could do any good. 'It's very nice,' she remarked, while his eyes stayed open, looking at the cream-painted blank ceiling of the ward. 'You couldn't be in a better place. I know they'll look after you, and I'll come twice a week to see you.'

'Aye,' he acknowledged, though out of it all.

'I've got to go now, love, or I'll miss the bus.'

At first there was nothing to do except keep the house clean. Polishing glass on the pictures, shining knives and forks, putting fresh paper on the kitchen shelves, she hoped his nervous breakdown wouldn't take too long to cure, though tears fell at the huge cannonball blow that had landed its weight against her: such mental things could last years. First Ivor gone, and now Fred; it was a bit bloody much. She cried to the empty house between sobs. She came in for sympathy from the neighbours: 'He was as good as gold,' a woman met shopping said, as if he'd already been buried and prayed over, 'but them's the sort that suffers first. It's a shame. Still, Mrs. Hargreaves, if there's anything I can do for you, duck, just let me know.'

The novelty of living alone wore off. She began to feel young again, but it was a different sort of youth to when, every Thursday during the war, she walked across the road with her allowance book to collect Fred's fourteen shillings from the post office. It was a lonely, thrilling sort of freedom that began to dawn. She begrudged the frequent visits of both families who thought she wanted to stay in a continual state of being cheered-up, and when she told all of them in a loud voice that this wasn't so, her own parents retired hoping that she, after all, wasn't going the same way as 'that poor Fred', while Fred's mother and father went away thinking they could see at last who had made their poor son the way he was.

Dates changed on each evening paper, and months passed. Men began noticing her in the street (or she noticed them noticing her again) giving looks which meant that they would like to get in bed with her. She found this far from agreeable, but it did hold back the full misery of Fred's incarceration from turning her into an old woman. Anyway, why shouldn't she feel pleased when men smiled or winked at her in passing? she thought, seeing that it had taken misfortune to make her realize how firm her figure was at the bust and hips, how smooth-skinned and pale her face under dark hair. These sentiments descended on her with as little warning as Fred's illness had on him. To everyone else she stuck it out like a widow waiting for her husband to come back from the grave.

Twice a week she took a bus through curving lanes to the sudden tower that dominated the camplike spread of lesser buildings. Getting off the bus with her bundles and magazines, flowers and grapes, and clean handkerchiefs with the odour of ironing still on them, she felt desolate at being one of so many, as if such numbers visiting sick-minded men and women made it a shameless and guilty job that fate had hooked them into, and that they should try and hide their own stupidity and bad luck from each other.

She hurried head down to be first in the ward, going along corridors whose low ceilings sported so many reptilian pipes that it seemed as if she was deep in one of those submarine ships seen on the pictures. She then entered a light-enough ward, to find a waxen spiritual embalming of her husband that even pins would not wake up.

'Fred,' she said, still on her feet and spreading gifts over the bed, 'I've brought you these.'

'Aye,' he answered, an affirmation used by their parents, which he had taken to since his illness.

'Fred, they tell me you'll be getting better soon.'

'Aye'—again.

'Did they give you them new drugs yet?'

'Aye.'

'As long as you don't get that shock treatment. Everything's O.K. at home. I'm managing all right.' She had to sit and look at him for an hour, because to leave before then, even though there was nothing left to say, was unthinkable. His mind might be a thousand miles away under his skin, but he'd remember it. She wondered what weird force had turned his life into a half sleep that she could no longer penetrate. He wasn't suffering, and that was a good job. Sometimes they saw snakes and dragons and screamed for hours, but Fred looked quiet enough, though there was no saying what he was like on days she didn't come. His brown calm eyes watched her, and she wondered if he still heard those morse codes he'd been so cranky on when they came from his expensive black radio. Of course, she nodded to her thoughts, that's what sent him, hearing those terrible squeaking messages night in and night out. Once, she had switched off the television and listened by Ivor's door, and to her the swift high-pitched dots and dashes had sounded like a monkey laughing —or trying to, which was worse. God knows what he made of such noise, and there was no way of finding out because he set fire to his papers every night, saying in his maddening know-all voice how wireless operators had to keep secret all messages they took down, otherwise it was prison for them. If she'd been the jealous sort she would have told him off about spending so much time at his wireless because, back from work, he could hardly wait to get his tea and a wash before he was up those stairs and glued to it. Still, most blokes would have been throwing their money away in a pub, and getting ulcers into the bargain. You can't have everything, and that was a fact, she supposed.

'I'll bring you a custard next week, love,' she said, wondering how else she could cheer him up.

'Aye.'

'If you want anything, drop me a postcard.' She didn't see him as helpless, treated him almost as if he had chosen to lie in that fashion and could come out of it at will—though from the way he smiled it was obvious he couldn't. In his locker were half a dozen paperback books she'd brought him, but she knew he hadn't read them. Still, they looked good in a place like this, and maybe he'd need them soon. You never knew when the steel band at the back of his eyes would snap and set him free again. She held his hand, shyly because many other visitors were in the ward, though they were too busy holding other hands to notice.

Always first into the hospital, she came out last, and so had to find a seat on the top deck of the bus, where pipe and cigarette smoke spread thickly. Surging, twisting movement was a relief—the bus eating its headlit way through winter's approaching darkness, speeding when the black canyon of trees straightened. She arched her back after the busy day, stared along the bus where other people talked out the highlights of their visit. Up to now her grief had been too new to allow for making friends, or do more than nod to a greeting, but when the man next to her asked:

'How was he today?' she replied:

'About the same,' and blushed as red as the sun which, hovering on the fields, resembled a beetroot going into the reverse of its existence, slipping back to the comfortable gloom of winter soil from which it had come. I'm a fool she thought, not daring to look. Why did I answer the cheeky devil like that? But she glanced at him, while his own eyes took in the bleak fall of night outside which, from his smile, made the bus interior feel like snug home to him. He was a young man who seemed born for nothing but work, awkward when his best clothes claimed their right to dominate him one day of the week. He was about thirty, she guessed, unmarried perhaps, since his approach was anything but furtive.

'It's a long job,' he said, 'once they get in a place like that. Longer than T.B. I reckon.'

'Well,' she said, thinking his face too red and healthy-

74

looking for him to be a collier, 'they wouldn't keep 'em in longer than they had to either, would they? Cost too much.'

He took out a cigarette and, in spite of her retort, the smoke didn't increase her annoyance, for his lighting-up was debonair, matched to the feel of his dressed-up best. A cigarette suited him more than a collar and tie, and she didn't doubt that a pint of ale would suit him even more. Maybe he's nervous, she smiled, underneath it all. 'I don't suppose they would,' he said, having taken his time over it.

'It ain't the sort of thing they die from, either,' she added.

'There's that to be thankful for. I'm sorry'—out came his twenty-packet again—'Smoke, duck?'

'No, thanks.' Who did he think he was? Who does he think I am, as well? 'Yes, I will have one.'

'I like a fag,' he said. 'Keeps me company.'

The opening was plain a mile off, but she refused it: 'Who do you see at the hospital, then?'

'A pal o' mine. He's in surgical though. Fell off some scaffolding last winter. He only broke an arm—that's what we thought, anyway—but he ain't been the same in the head since. He's an Irish bloke, a paddy, you know, and none of his family get to see him, so me and the lads tek turns at having half a day off to see he's all right. Shovel in a few fags and things. Be out in a couple o' months, according to the doctor.'

She hardly listened. 'You're a brickie, then?'

'Brickie's labourer. Who do *you* go and see? I mek good money though.'

'My husband.' At Redhill the lights of Nottingham blistered the sky in front, drew them down to its welcoming horseshoe. His naïve glance seemed too good, and she wondered if such an expression weren't the ultimate extension of his guile. 'I shan't be sorry to get home,' she told him. 'It's a long day, coming all this way.'

The frown left his face as soon as he thought she might see it: 'You can spend too much time at home. I like staying out, having a good time.'

She saw where his glance went, and began to fasten her coat. 'There is something to be said for it, I suppose.'

'There is, an' all,' he grinned.

'It's a long time since I had a drink,' she claimed, self-righteousness seeming the only defence left.

'Come and have one with me then, before you go home. You'll enjoy it.'

She flushed: he thinks I'm trying to knock on with him, and the idea made her so angry that she said, though not too loud in case she was heard and shown-up more for the flirt she might seem to be: 'What you want is a smack across the face.'

'I suppose so.' His voice verged on sadness. 'I'm sorry if I offended you, duck. But come and have a drink with me, then we can make it up.'

He was the limit. 'What do you tek me for?'—a question that puzzled him since it was too early to say. 'In any case,' she told him, 'I'm married, respectably married.'

'So am I,' he answered, 'but I'm not narrow-minded'—then kept his trap shut while the bus went slowly through bright lights and traffic, stopping and starting like possible future answers formulating in Nan's mind in case he had the nerve to speak again.

At the terminus they filed out onto the asphalt, and when he repeated his proposition in the darker shadows of the station yard both were shocked at the unequivocal 'yes' that for a few seconds kept them apart, then pulled them passionately together.

IV

Fred's brainstorm thinned-out at a predictable speed, leaving an unclouded blue-sea vision of a mind from which the large ship had slid away. He walked out of the ward with a suitcase in one hand and a morning paper tucked under the other arm. His fervent kiss irritated Nan, but all she could say was: 'You'll be better off at home.'

'I know I shall. And I'll never want to leave it again love.' He stared with pleasure at the lush green of middle spring, the febrile smell of grass and catkins beating petrol smells through the open bus-window. Water charged under the lane, into an enormous pipe, a swollen silver arm speckling a field that cows drank from. He rubbed sun from his eyes as if after a fair spell in prison, was too absorbed in his journey to say much, enjoying his way out and back, Nan thought, as she herself had revelled in his absence once the shock of breakdown had worn off.

The first bungalows lay like tarted-up kennels over suburban fields, and he turned from them: 'I feel good, love. I feel marvellous.'

She smiled. 'I thought you did. You look as though you've had a long holiday.'

'I suppose it was, in a way.' He took her hand and squeezed it: 'Let's go down town this afternoon. Go for a stroll round, then spend a couple of hours at the pictures. We can have a real holiday between now and Monday.'

'All right'—doubting that they would.

As he walked down the yard, the neighbours thought him another of Nan's fancy men who had gone into the house via back door late at night in the last months, and slid out of the front door early next morning. She had been sly about it, but not sly enough, they grinned. Not that Fred was in danger of being informed, for it was hard to imagine him pasting her: she was beyond that by now, and in any case he would never be man enough for it. And when he did find out—as he must in time—then there'd be no point in knocking her about for what had become history.

They had to look twice before recognizing the Fred they'd known for years. His sallow face had filled out, and he had lost the lively movements of his brown eyes that, through not being sure of themselves, had given and received sufficient warmth and sympathy to make him popular. His best suit would have shown as too tight if Nan hadn't thought to take his mac which, having always been slightly too big, hid the worst of his weight increase from curious eyes. Most obvious was his face, which had broadened. The expression of it was firmly tainted by middle age, though the neighbours were to swear how much better he looked, and what a lot of good the country air had done. 'It's fattened him,' they said, 'and it'll turn out to have fattened her as well—though it wasn't fresh air and good food as did that.' Fred caught their laughter by the back door.

The smells of the yard were familiar, tea-leaves and coal dust, car fuel and midday stew. He revelled in it, couldn't wait to get back to work next Monday and walk among those hot, oilburning machines which would make his homecoming complete. Nan hung up his mac, while he turned to the living-room. He thought they'd walked into the wrong house. 'What's this, then?'

'What's what?' She smiled at his frown, though it seemed like insult to her: 'What's what, Fred?'

'All this'—waving his arm, as if it indicated something that wasn't worth a light. He shifted his stance, uncomfortable at the change that had taken place while he was away.

'Don't you like it?'

'It's all right,' he. conceded after a pause. 'It's a surprise though.'

'Aye.' He looked carefully, again. The old furniture, the old wallpaper, the old curtains and pictures—all gone, swept away by a magic wand of six dead months. The room was brighter, stippled green-contemporary and (though this didn't occur to them) resembled more the hospital he had just left than the previous homely decoration of their married life. 'You don't like it, then?'

He saw a thundercloud-quarrel looming up, and only ten minutes back from the hospital. 'It's lighter. Yes, I reckon it's O.K. It's marvellous, in fact.'

'Thanks,' she said. 'I thought you'd jump for joy. I'll make you a cup of tea now.'

'It must have cost a good bit,' he called into the scullery, losing some of his strangeness at being home.

'I spent my football money on it,' she said. 'All but a few quid.'

'I suppose that's how you was able to look after me so well, bring me things every time.'

'It was,' she said.

'And I thought it was because you was such a good manager.'

'Don't be sarcastic. I often wondered what I'd do with it, you know that, and now you can see. I suppose you think I'm a dope, blowing it on the house when you spent your share on yourself, on a . . . wireless set. Well, I expect I am, but I like to keep the home nice. As long as you've got a pleasant place to live in there ain't much as can happen to you.'

'That's true.'

'Takes work and money though to keep it going, but it's worth it. Not that there's owt wrong with work.'

He stood by the fire, drinking his first cup of tea: 'You can say that again. I'll be glad to clock-in on Monday.'

'It's what makes people live,' she went on, almost happily, he thought, 'and you as well, if I know you. You've always been a lad for work. Course, after a while there gets as if there's not enough for a woman to do when she's got no kids. That's why most women in my position should be in a factory. No good moping around all day, or gossiping, or just sitting by the fire pulling a meagrim because you've read all the books at the library. You need a proper job. You can fit your housework in easy enough, and let them as say you can't come to your house and prove it.'

'What are you going on like this for, then?' he cried.

'Because I'm going to start work as well on Monday, at my old firm.'

Knowing what her game was, he became calmer. 'Maybe they don't need anybody.' They sat for a meal: cold ham, fresh salad and bread, sardines, a porkpie each in a cellophane wrapper. 'I went the other day to see 'em. They'd love to have me back, as an overlooker as well. The processing hasn't altered a bit since I was last there.'

He smiled: 'It wouldn't, not in a hundred years, no more than it would where I work.'

'I'll be like a fish back in water after an hour or two,' she exulted. 'I didn't tell 'em I'd only be there about three months, though while I am I'll put a bit of money by.'

'We don't need money,' he said, his appetite failing,

'because we'll be all right when I've pulled in a few wage-packets.'

'Not as I see it. We'll want all we can get, because I'm pregnant.'

He smiled, then the smile ran from his face before the claws of her meaning savaged it. 'Pregnant?'

'Yes,' she said. 'Can't you see it? My belly's up. We'll have a kid in the house in six months. You won't know the place.' She glared, as if hoping he'd try denying it. But the healthy bloom of fresh air had already left his cheeks. 'You've got things fixed up, then, haven't you?'

'Things often fix themselves up, whatever you do.' Her heartbeats were visible, breasts lifting and falling, making it seem to him as if her blouse were alive.

'Whose kid is it?'

'Nobody's as matters.'

He trembled the teacup back into its saucer. 'It matters to me, it bloody-well does.'

'We can have another kid between us after this, so you needn't carry on.'

He stood from his half-finished meal. 'That's what you think. You're a lunatic'—and his slow intimidating tread of disappointment on the stairs filled her more with sorrow for him than for herself.

She hadn't expected him to cave-in so deeply at the first telling, hoped he would argue, settle what had to be settled before going off to soothe his injuries in solitude. 'Maybe I am a lunatic'—and though she never imagined he lacked guts for such a vital set-to, it could be that she'd accepted too blindly the advice that things have a way of working them-selves out better than you expect—given by Danny on telling him she was pregnant, and before he lit off for a new con-struction job at Rotherham. She remembered him saying, after their first night together, that whenever he met a woman the first thing that crossed his mind was 'If I have a kid by her, which of us will it look like?' 'And is that what you thought about me when you started talking to me on the bus?' 'What do you think?' he'd laughed. 'Of course it was, you juicy

80

little piece.' But now he'd gone, and only she would be able to see how the kid turned out. Maybe that was why he wondered—because he knew he'd never be there to see. The bloody rotter—though there wasn't much else he could have done but hopped-it. Still, (her sigh was a sad one), the last few months had been heaven, a wild spree on what was left from her football money. She'd boozed and sang with Danny, in a pub tucked somewhere in the opposite end of town. It was a long while since she'd laughed so much, played darts and argued with the young men (some no older than teddy boys) all earning fair money at Gedling pit and out for a good time while they could get it. She'd never imagined her pool winnings would come in so handy, had even taken to filling coupons in again, which she and Fred had sworn never to do once they cleared a packet. Getting home at night she had felt Danny's hands and lips loving her: warm and ready for him, she came alive once more as the sweet shock of orgasm twisted her body. She hadn't bargained on getting pregnant, but couldn't feel sorry either, in spite of Fred clattering about upstairs. She'd hoped that the bliss of his absence would turn into the heaven of his coming back, but that had been too much to hope for, like most things. Tears forced a way out. Thoughts of Fred and their past life were too vivid and accurate now. 'I couldn't help it,' she said. 'I didn't want to have anything to do with Danny, but I wasn't myself.' She'd often forgot Fred's existence, her mind withdrawing to a time even before meeting him, a sense of paradise so far distant that she'd sometimes write on a postcard: VISIT HOSPITAL TOMORROW and lean it against the clock, so as not to lose him altogether.

There seemed no doubt to Fred upstairs that an end was reached but, seeing his half-filled suit-case on a chair, the end was like a sheer smooth wall blocking a tunnel in which there wasn't room enough to turn round and grope for a new beginning, though that seemed the only hope.

The fag-end nipped his fingers, fell and he let his foot slide over it. In the darkness of the cupboard he saw pictures of his London journey that afternoon, a long packed train rattling him to some strange impersonal bedroom smelling of trainsmoke and damp, and a new job, struggle, solitude, and even less reason for living than he had now. Still, there's not much for it but to get out. The moves of his departure were slow, but he smiled and told himself there was no hurry.

Ivor's toys had gone, cleared away by Nan after he'd been carted-off that morning. The jig-saw made sense, showed her returning alone from the hospital and not knowing what to do because he, Fred, was no longer part of the house. He saw himself smashing Ivor's toys by boot and hand, a lunatic flailing after a brainstorm harvest too abundant of life and energy.

Something half-concealed by a piece of clean sacking flashed into the back door of his eye before turning away from the cupboard. Pulling it clear he saw the radio set, black, deathly, and switched off, lying like some solid reproachful monster in place of the dustbinned toys. He grinned: Nan had intended hiding it where she imagined he was unlikely to see it, and he wondered why she hadn't scrapped it with the toys. He knelt towards the eyes and dials, touching and spinning in the hope that agreeable noises would lift from it.

Its size and dignity was intimidating, made him stand back and view it from a point where it disturbed him less. The vision began as half a memory striving to enter his brain. It edged a way sharply in. He laughed at it, tapped a pleasant hollow-sounding noise on the lid with his fingers, not like an army drum but something more satisfying, primitive and jungle-like. It reminded him of Peter Nkagwe, whose illuminated face was locked like stone as he battered out messages hour after hour in the signals office years ago.

The black box weighed a hundred pounds. Two hands flexed and stretched over it, pressing the sharp rim into his groin as he moved, breathless and foot by foot. His dark hair fell forward, joined beads of sweat in pricking his skin. Hospital had made him soft, but he resisted shifting the radio in two stages, found enough strength to do it the hard way, drawing on the rock-middle of himself to reach the table at one agonizing go, and set it so delicately down it would have been impossible either to see or hear the soundless contact of wood and metal.

It was a minute's work to screw on aerial and power, slick in earphones and switch a current-flow through valves and superhet. Energy went like an invisible stoat into each purple and glowing filament. The panels lit up and background static began as if, when a child, he had pressed a sea-shell to his ear and heard the far-off poise and fall of breakers at Skegness; then such subtlety went, and noise rose to the loud electric punching of a full-grown sea in continual motion. He turned the volume down and sent the fly-wheel onto morse code.

The sea calmed for its mundane messages of arrival and departure, of love and happy birthday and grandma died and I bought presents in Bombay, and from this festive liner—white, sleek and grandiose—once more seen between clear sky and otherwise desolate flat sea—signals were emitted saying that a son had been (or was it would be?) born with love from Nancy in a place where both were doing well.

He slung the pencil down and stared at the accidental words, grew a smile at the irony of the message. He frowned, as if a best friend taunted him. The calm boat flowed on and a voice spoke over his shoulder: 'What have you got there, Fred?'

'A message,' he answered, not looking round, sliding his hand over so that she wouldn't see it. 'I take them down from ships at sea.'

'I know you do.'

'All sorts of things,' he added, sociable without knowing why. The earphones fell to his neck and he needle-spun the wavelength, a noise that reminded Nancy of running by the huge Arboretum birdcages as a kid: 'What though?'

'Telegrams and things. Ordinary stuff. Listen to what this funny one says'—sliding his hand away—' "FRED HARGREAVES LEFT HOME AT ONE O'CLOCK THURSDAY AFTERNOON." '

She turned: 'You're not going, Fred, are you? I don't believe it.'

'That's what the telegram said. Everyone I take down says the same thing. I can't get over it.'

'Talk proper,' she cried. 'It's not right to go off like this.'

He laughed, a grinding of heart and soul. 'In't it?'

'What about your job?'

'There's plenty more where that came from.'

'What about me?'

He laid his earphones down, and spoke with exaggerated awful quietness. 'You should a thought of that before you trolloped off and got a bastard in you.'

'It's all finished now. Didn't I tell you? It's about time you believed me.'

'You told me a lot of things.' It was more of a grouse than a reproach. 'All on 'em lies.'

'I thought it was better that way.'

'And going with that bloke? Was that better as well?' His shout startled her, brown eyes glittering under darkening shadows, as if his exhaustion had never been lifted by a sojourn at the hospital. Neighbours from next door and out in the yard could hear them shouting. Don't tell me he's found out already. Well, well!

She was still in the new dress worn to fetch him home, and it showed already a slight thickness at the waist. 'I couldn't help it,' she cried, able to add, in spite of tears on her face: 'Anyway, what did you expect? We'd had no life between us since Ivor died. I was fed up on it. I had to let myself go.'

'It was too bad though, worn't it?'

'I'm not saying it wasn't. But I'm not going to go on bended knees and ask you to stay. I'm not an' all.' She stiffened, looked at him with hatred: 'It's as much your fault as mine.'

'I'm leaving,' he said, 'I'm off.'

'Go on, then.' Her face turned, the tone mechanical and meant, the quiet resignation of it a hot poker burning through his eyes. It was a final torment he could not take. Dazed by the grief of her decision she didn't see his hand coming. A huge blow, like a boulder flying at top speed in a gale, hit the side of her face, threw her back, feet collapsing. Another fist caught her, and another. She crashed on to the bed, a cry of shock beating her to it there. As she was to tell her mother: 'He hadn't hit me before then, and he wain't hit me again, either. Maybe I deserved it, though.'

He tore the message off and screwed it tight, flung it to the far corner of the room. Then he went to Nan and tried to comfort her, the iron hooves of desperate love trampling them back into the proportions of matrimonial life.

THE BIKE

The Easter I was fifteen I sat at the table for supper and Mam said to me: 'I'm glad you've left school. Now you can go to work.'

'I don't want to go to wok,' I said in a big voice.

'Well, you've got to,' she said. 'I can't afford to keep a pit-prop like yo' on nowt.'

I sulked, pushed my toasted cheese away as if it was the worst kind of slop. 'I thought I could have a break before starting.'

'Well you thought wrong. You'll be out of harm's way at work.' She took my plate and emptied it on John's, my younger brother's, knowing the right way to get me mad. That's the trouble with me: I'm not clever. I could have bashed our John's face in and snatched it back, except the little bastard had gobbled it up, and Dad was sitting by the fire, behind his paper with one tab lifted. 'You can't get me out to wok quick enough, can you?' was all I could say at Mam.

Dad chipped in, put down his paper. 'Listen: no wok, no grub. So get out and look for a job tomorrow, and don't come back till you've got one.'

Going to the bike factory to ask for a job meant getting up early, just as if I was back at school; there didn't seem any point in getting older. My old man was a good worker though, and I knew in my bones and brain that I took after him. At the school garden the teacher used to say: 'Colin, you're the best worker I've got, and you'll get on when you leave'—after I'd spent a couple of hours digging spuds while all the others had been larking about trying to run each other over with the lawn-rollers. Then the teacher would sell the spuds off at threepence a pound and what did I get out of it? Bogger-all. Yet I liked the work because it wore me out; and I always feel pretty good when I'm worn out.

I knew you had to go to work though, and that rough work was best. I saw a picture once about a revolution in Russia, about the workers taking over and everything (like Dad wants to) and they lined everybody up and made them hold their hands out and the working blokes went up and down looking at them. Anybody whose hands was lily-white was taken away and shot. The others was O.K. Well, if ever that happened in this country, I'd be O.K., and that made me feel better when a few days later I was walking down the street in overalls at half-past seven in the morning with the rest of them. One side of my face felt lively and interested in what I was in for, but the other side was crooked and sorry for itself, so that a neighbour got a front view of my whole clock and called with a wide laugh, a gap I'd like to have seen a few inches lower down—in her neck: 'Never mind, Colin, it ain't all that bad.'

The man on the gate took me to the turnery. The noise hit me like a boxing-glove as I went in, but I kept on walking straight into it without flinching, feeling it reach right into my guts as if to wrench them out and use them as garters. I was handed over to the foreman; then the foreman passed me on to the toolsetter; and the toolsetter took me to another youth—so that I began to feel like a hot wallet.

The youth led me to a cupboard, opened it, and gave me a sweeping brush. 'Yo' do that gangway,' he said, 'and I'll do this one.' My gangway was wider, but I didn't bother to mention it. 'Bernard,' he said, holding out his hand, 'that's me. I go on a machine next week, a drill.'

'How long you been on this sweeping?' I wanted to know, bored with it already.

'Three months. Every lad gets put on sweeping first, just to get 'em used to the place.' Bernard was small and thin, older than me. We took to each other. He had round bright eyes and dark wavy hair, and spoke in a quick way as if he'd stayed at school longer than he had. He was idle, and I thought him sharp and clever, maybe because his mam and dad died when he was three. He'd been brought up by an asthmatic auntie who'd not only spoiled him but let him run wild as well, he told me later when we sat supping from our tea mugs. He'd quietened down now though, and butter wouldn't melt in his mouth, he said with a wink. I couldn't think why this was, after all his stories about him being a mad-head—which put me off him at first, though after a bit he was my mate, and that was that.

We was talking one day, and Bernard said the thing he wanted to buy most in the world was a gram and lots of jazz records—New Orleans style. He was saving up and had already got ten quid.

'Me,' I said, 'I want a bike, to get out at week-ends up Trent. A shop on Arkwright Street sells good 'uns second hand.'

I went back to my sweeping. It was a fact I've always wanted a bike. Speed gave me a thrill. Malcolm Campbell was my bigshot—but I'd settle for a two-wheeled pushbike. I'd once borrowed my cousin's and gone down Balloon House Hill so quick I passed a bus. I'd often thought how easy it would be to pinch a bike: look in a shop window until a bloke leaves his bike to go into the same shop, then nip in just before him and ask for something you knew they hadn't got; then walk out whistling to the bike at the kerb and ride off as if it's yours while the bloke's still in the shop. I'd brood for hours: fly home on it, enamel it, file off the numbers, turn the handlebars round, change the pedals, take lamps off or put them on . . . only, no, I thought, I'll be honest and save up for one when I get forced out to work, worse luck.

But work turned out to be a better life than school. I kept as hard at it as I could, and got on well with the blokes because I used to spout about how rotten the wages was and how hard the bosses slaved us—which made me popular you can bet. Like my old man always says, I told them: 'At home, when you've got a headache, mash a pot of tea. At work, when you've got a headache, strike.' Which brought a few laughs.

Bernard was put on his drill, and one Friday while he was cleaning it down I stood waiting to cart his rammel off. 'Are you still saving up for that bike, then?' he asked, pushing steel dust away with a handbrush.

'Course I am. But I'm a way off getting one yet. They rush you a fiver at that shop. Guaranteed, though.'

He worked on for a minute or two then, as if he'd got a birthday present or was trying to spring a good surprise on me, said without turning round: 'I've made up my mind to sell my bike.'

'I didn't know~you'd got one.'

'Well'—a look on his face as if there was a few things I didn't know—'I bus it to work: it's easier.' Then in a pallier voice: 'I got it last Christmas, from my auntie. But I want a record player now.'

My heart was thumping. I knew I hadn't got enough, but: 'How much do you want for it?'

He smiled. 'It ain't how much I want for the bike, it's how much more dough I need to get the gram and a couple of discs.'

I saw Trent Valley spread out below me from the top of Carlton Hill—fields and villages, and the river like a white scarf dropped from a giant's neck. 'How much do you need, then?'

He took his time about it, as if still having to reckon it up. 'Fifty bob.' I'd only got two quid—so the giant snatched his scarf away and vanished. Then Bernard seemed in a hurry to finish the deal: 'Look, I don't want to mess about, I'll let it go for two pounds five. You can borrow the other five bob.'

'I'll do it then,' I said, and Bernard shook my hand like he was going away in the army. 'It's a deal. Bring the dough in the morning, and I'll bike it to wok.'

Dad was already in when I got home, filling the kettle at the scullery tap. I don't think he felt safe without there was a kettle on the gas. 'What would you do if the world suddenly ended, Dad?' I once asked when he was in a good mood. 'Mash some tea and watch it,' he said. He poured me a cup.

'Lend's five bob, Dad, till Friday.'

He slipped the cosy on. 'What do you want to borrow money for?' I told him. 'Who from?' he asked.

'My mate at wok.'

He passed me the money. 'Is it a good 'un?'

'I ain't seen it yet. He's bringing it in the morning.'

'Make sure the brakes is safe.'

Bernard came in half an hour late, so I wasn't able to see the bike till dinner-time. I kept thinking he'd took bad and wouldn't come at all, but suddenly he was stooping at the door to take his clips off—so's I'd know he'd got his—my—bike. He looked paler than usual, as if he'd been up the canal-bank all night with a piece of skirt and caught a bilious-bout. I paid him at dinner-time. 'Do you want a receipt for it?' he laughed. It was no time to lark about. I gave it a short test around the factory, then rode it home.

The next three evenings, for it was well in to summer, I rode a dozen miles out into the country, where fresh air smelt like cowshit and the land was coloured different, was wide open and windier than in streets. Marvellous. It was like a new life starting up, as if till then I'd been tied by a mile long rope round the ankle to home. Whistling along lanes I planned trips to Skegness, wondering how many miles I could make in a whole day. If I pedalled like mad, bursting my lungs for fifteen hours I'd reach London where I'd never been. It was like sawing through the bars in clink. It was a good bike as well, a few years old, but a smart racer with lamps and saddle-bag and a pump that went. I thought Bernard was a bit loony parting with it at that price, but I supposed that that's how blokes are when they get dead set on a gram and discs. They'd sell their own mother, I thought, enjoying a mad dash down from Canning Circus, weaving between the cars for kicks.

'What's it like, having a bike?' Bernard asked, stopping to slap me on the back—as jolly as I'd ever seen him, yet in a kind of way that don't happen between pals.

'You should know,' I said. 'Why? It's all right, ain't it? The wheels are good, aren't they?'

An insulted look came into his eyes. 'You can give it back if you like. I'll give you your money.'

'I don't want it,' I said. I could no more part with it than my right arm, and he knew it. 'Got the gram yet?' And he told me about it for the next half-hour. It had got so many dials for this and that he made it sound like a space ship. We was both satisfied, which was the main thing.

That same Saturday I went to the barber's for my monthly D.A. and when I came out I saw a bloke getting on my bike to ride it away. I tagged him on the shoulder, my fist flashing red for danger.

'Off,' I said sharp, ready to smash the thieving bastard. He turned to me. A funny sort of thief, I couldn't help thinking, a respectable-looking bloke of about forty wearing glasses and shiny shoes, smaller than me, with a moustache. Still, the swivel-eyed sinner was taking my bike.

'I'm boggered if I will,' he said, in a quiet way so that I thought he was a bit touched. 'It's my bike, anyway.'

'It bloody-well ain't,' I swore, 'and if you don't get off I'll crack you one.'

A few people gawked at us. The bloke didn't mess about and I can understand it now. 'Missis,' he called, 'just go down the road to that copperbox and ask a policeman to come up 'ere, will you? This is my bike, and this young bogger nicked it.'

I was strong for my age. 'You sodding fibber,' I cried, pulling him clean off the bike so's it clattered to the pavement. I picked it up to ride away, but the bloke got me round the waist, and it was more than I could do to take him off up the road as well, even if I wanted to. Which I didn't.

'Fancy robbing a working-man of his bike,' somebody called out from the crowd of idle bastards now collected. I could have mowed them down.

But I didn't get a chance. A copper came, and the man was soon flicking out his wallet, showing a bill with the number of the bike on it: proof right enough. But I still thought he'd made a mistake. 'You can tell us all about that at the Guildhall,' the copper said to me.

I don't know why—I suppose I want my brains testing—but I stuck to a story that I found the bike dumped at the end of the yard that morning and was on my way to give it in at a copshop, and had called for a haircut first. I think the magistrate half believed me, because the bloke knew to the minute when it was pinched, and at that time I had a perfect alibi—I was in work, proved by my clocking-in card. I knew some rat who hadn't been in work though when he should have been.

All the same, being found with a pinched bike, I got put on probation, and am still doing it. I hate old Bernard's guts for playing a trick like that on me, his mate. But it was lucky for him I hated the coppers more and wouldn't nark on anybody, not even a dog. Dad would have killed me if ever I had, though he didn't need to tell me. I could only thank God a story came to me as quick as it did, though in one way I still sometimes reckon I was barmy not to have told them how I got the bike.

There's one thing I do know. I'm waiting for Bernard to come out of borstal. He got picked up, the day after I was copped with the bike, for robbing his auntie's gas meter to buy more discs. She'd had about all she could stand from him, and thought a spell inside would do him good, if not cure him altogether. I've got a big bone to pick with him, because he owes me forty-five bob. I don't care where he gets it—even if he goes out and robs another meter—but I'll get it out of him, I swear blind I will. I'll pulverise him.

Another thing about him though that makes me laugh is that, if ever there's a revolution and everybody's lined-up with their hands out, Bernard's will still be lily-white, because he's a bone-idle thieving bastard—and then we'll see how he goes on; because mine won't be lily-white, I can tell you that now. And you never know, I might even be one of the blokes picking 'em out.

TO BE COLLECTED

Donnie came out of the snackshack in Heanor marketplace, paused to wipe crumbs from his mouth with a damp sleeve of raincoat. 'Belt-up, you rag-bags,' he shouted, to his two brothers beckoning from their government surplus lorry.

He ploughed into waterpuddles, socks and flesh soaked. 'Can't you see I'm coming?' Now look at what they've made me do! Curses ate into him like a corkscrew—'I'm wet through now. I'll catch me death o' cold. You poxed-up bastards,' he raved, a fist pushed further into his groin pocket when he'd like it to be out and slamming them. He broke his tirade to grin at a couple of wide-eyed shopping women who thought he might have less dirty talk. 'Can't you wait a bit? You must have drainpipes, not guts, swallowing scorched tea like that.'

Tall Dave leaned out of the cab. His rawboned face, and grizzle-grey hair topped by a faded cap, jutted over a little boy pushing a tricycle. 'There ain't all day. We want to get cracking to Eastwood, see what we can get'—his voice raised but reasonable. Back inside he lit a cigarette, shifted to the middle: 'Hudge up. Flaptabs wants to park hissen.'

Bert, foot on the clutch and revving up loud, pressed himself against the door. He was the driver so, though the youngest of the three brothers, held the balance of which-way-turn and what-snackbar-stop decisions. He'd worked some time at the pitface, but too many changes of temperature, dampness and water, had marked him with pleurisy, menaced him with TB. Illness was shameful and unmanly, neither to be tolerated nor surrendered to, so he opted while sound for an outdoor life. This situation made him even more violent and morbid, see-sawed between pessimism, and hilarious pipe-dreams which came to nothing because he was so busy earning a living, though at the same time they enabled him to face making one.

'It's pissing down,' Donnie observed, installing himself in the warm, smoke-filled cab.

'Do you good,' Bert said, changing gear, 'get you a wash.'

'You can't beat a drop o' rain,' Donnie said, 'keeps 'em home for when the ragman calls.' He'd been involved in the last few days, in sporadic argument with Bert, though he'd given signs of wanting to pack it in without losing pride: 'I 'ad a wash this morning before I came out, which is more than yo' did, our Bert, you blackfaced bastard'—he grinned from his perished, intense face.

Dave hated argument: 'Why don't you two stop fucking-well needling each other? I'm not kidding, but you're driving me off my bleddy nut, day in and day out.' Neither took him up on this so, map reading, systematic and sharp for detail, he said: 'Left at the market then, out o' these crowds. Watch you don't hit that post office van—or you might accidentally knock-off a few thousand postal orders.'

'If I did it'd be enough to keep us for a year at the wage we mek.' Bert took Dave's directions smoothly, as if thinking them out for himself.

As the eldest Dave felt it his right to give orders, though he was careful to modify his voice and phrases when doing so. 'Get round this corner and we'll head for Eastwood. We've got to call at them houses we left hand-bills at this morning.' An old man, macless and without umbrella, shuffled off the pavement. 'I'll run that old bastard down,' Bert said. 'Can't see a foot before 'im.' He cupped a hand to his mouth: 'Get off home and DIE!'

'Less to feed,' Donnie laughed, no longer the butt-end of their fun: 'Don't hit him, though.'

'Listen at old soft-heart,' Bert jeered.

Dave agreed: 'Wappy bleeder'—scornful because they obviously wouldn't run the man over, and because Donnie's sympathy reminded them that they daren't. Able to cross between studs, the old man held his pace and shambled to-wards safe pavement. 'Join the army,' Bert shouted. 'They're crying out for blokes like yo', dad!' The man turned. A worn white death-mask of a starvo face opened into a smile. He shook his fist and stood on the pavement laughing.

They waved back. They all laughed, and the lorry shot forward. Shop awnings were pelted by violent rain: 'Whose idea was it to come out today?' he moaned, a side-glance at Donnie. 'Shaking it down in buckets and nowt between us and getting into debt but the price o' five fags and a gallon o' petrol. What a life. Out on the road in all this weltering piss.' He grumbled with a deadpan face, drew back his gears to the pitchdown of a steep hill, going fast between houses and towards a railway on the valley bottom, scarves of mist and black smoke boiling from pit-chimneys and train funnels. 'I wouldn't live out 'ere for a pension.'

'Go on,' Donnie cried, the optimist who, even in the most terrible glasshouse of the British Army, averred that things might have been worse in a German deathcamp, and that pig-swill was better than no swill at all. 'We might strike lucky at Eastwood, with an old copper or a mangle. Or an old firegrate. A few stone o' woollens. You never know.'

'All we'll get,' Bert prophesied, 'is a couple of bugged-up bedticks that a consumptive man and wife have just pegged out on. We'll be lucky to get eighteen pence the two: a cup of tea and a bun each.'

'That wain't keep my gang o' kids,' Donnie put it. 'But we'll get more than that though, yo' see.'

'I don't know why you have so many kids, Donnie. I don't, honest. You know you can't afford to keep 'em.'

'They don't tek any bread out o' your mouth.' Donnie's family was a great consolation to him, and though he could understand why it was made a joke of by his brothers, he had never been able to see the justice of it. His face steeled hard: 'And I do keep 'em though, don't I, eh?'

'Well,' Dave killed the joke before it went too far, 'even me and Alice don't get enough to live on.'

'You might just as well put your head in the gas-oven and be done wi' it,' Bert said.

'That wouldn't do, either,' Donnie smiled. 'You've got no

right to talk like that. No use dying, is it?' Bert's eyes half closed at Donnie spinning things out to such a dead-end conclusion and, turning a corner, he roared into his ear:

'Wrap up. Brainless bastard'—so loud that even above the engine noise a policeman heard its subhuman command and glared into the cab to see what was the matter. Dave's eyes flashed out a picture of what possessions sprawled on the open back: A coil of rope, heap of sacks, and a folded tarpaulin that covered nothing because it had been fine when they set out. Everything soaked. But nothing for the copper to get big ideas at either. The eyes of the law swivelled out of sight. 'You want to be careful what you say,' Donnie called. 'I'm a few years older than yo', you know.'

Bert became solemn, then melancholy, and gave himself up to grandiose dreams as he held the lorry fast to an uphill shove into Eastwood. 'I'd like to build eight machine-guns into this vehicle—into the bonnet—and blast my way through owt as stood in our way,' he said with a laugh, slowing at MAJOR ROAD AHEAD. 'To blast coppers, that's what I'd use it for.'

'What about the Blackshirts?' Donnie said. 'They're coppers, aren't they?'

'Who's talking about Blackshirts? Shurrup.'

'Course they are,' Dave told him.

'One 'ud put his hand out to get my licence'—Bert went on, grinning, 'six on 'em at a roadblock, and I'd slow down a bit, as if I was all for the law and going to stop.'

'To give 'em a Woodbine out of the ten thousand we'd got in the back?'

He pulled a face at Donnie. 'So I'd press this specially built-in button, and hear them bullet-belts starting to move under our feet, and the road in front would get churned up and go all grey and black, and the lorry would go bump-bump over the rubble we'd made of everything, and we'd all laugh together at six coppers snuffing it behind.'

'Well,' Dave said, winking towards Donnie, 'you'd get summonsed then if you killed 'em, I know you would.'

'That's what used to 'appen in Chicago though,' Bert put in.

'Like in them old pictures, with James Cagney and George Raft.'

'Well'—from Donnie—'it don't 'appen anywhere now.'

'Not even in Russia,' Bert laughed. 'Like it did in that revolution.'

Donnie turned serious: 'If you did such a thing there now you'd end up filling saltbags, in the geranium mines.' And their laughter exploded, louder than any bomb or gunfire.

Eastwood was wetter than Heanor. They ascended the hill, patrolled rows of drenched uniform houses, desolate and scruffy at the backs, scruffier when TV aerials lifted Martian claws above slate-roofs and chimney stacks. Children were in school, and no one else seemed out on such a day. 'Pull up,' Dave rapped out. 'Let's get cracking on a couple o' these streets.'

'Maybe somebody's left a crust o' bread for us, or a clap-rag,' Bert scoffed, drawing into the kerb. 'I'll bet we don't see the sweat off a gnat's knackers—nor even as much as an old gas-stove.' Donnie caught on to this further wave of descending gloom, kept his monkey-face glum and silent. The lorry stayed by the kerb before any of them had the stomach to get out: the smell of their cigarettes and bodies made an atmosphere of homely warmth that they were loth to leave for wet unwelcoming backyards. 'It ain't all that bad,' Dave retorted to Bert's bitter weighing-up of their prospects, reaching under the steering-wheel for a pack of newly printed handbills. 'Before the war it was, but not since. Course, everything still looks the same.'

'And smells the same.'

'But all the colliers is on full time.'

'For a bit, anyway.'

Bert laughed. 'Everybody's got dough but us, I know that much.' For a moment their thoughts and voices had met in harmony, but drew away again when Donnie demanded: 'We got the lorry, ain't we?'

'Well'—Bert turned as if to rub the nub-end into his face—'we wokked for it, din't we?' It was impossible to deny this triumphant assertion, and all three brooded for a minute on the months of monstrous overtime in the summer as brickies' labourers on the new estates—heaving highloaded hods on bony shoulders, unstacking fresh-baked bricks from lorry-backs and hosing them down, lugging cement bags in the sun, lips cracking under hot tea and the blinding heat of shaving fires—a nightmare that nevertheless made a good memory in this wet daylight of a Monday morning—and which ended each with a hundred pounds to club-in for their rag-and-bone lorry. Dave glared savagely at the top handbill:

EX-SERVICEMAN'S COLLECTION
We give good CASH for
GAS-STOVES MANGLES LEAD
METALS OF ANY DESCRIPTION
RAGS AND BEDSTEADS
EVERYTHING
gratefully received
WE
call back in half an hour
THANK YOU.

'A lot o' bleeding good that does us,' Bert said, digging at Dave, whose idea the handbills had been. 'If we don't start making some money I'm going back to labouring.'

Dave groaned. They had discussed chucking it in before, but he prevailed on optimist Donnie to wield the casting vote that kept them at it. 'What's up with you? We made ten quid a-piece last week. You can't expect to get a millionaire's whack the first few months can you? Or p'raps you like working for a bleeding gaffer? I don't. I've 'ad enough o' that. You've only got to pull out a fag and you get your cards. Or see whether or not you backed a winner at dinner-time. You can bogger that for a lark. I'm not going to chuck it yet. I'd give it a longer try and see what we can do.' He reached for the map: 'We'll try Bolsover next week. The trouble with these places near Nottingham is they've allus bin done by some graballing bastard half an hour before; but up there, nobody ever bothers.'

'Like that place last week,' Bert thought, cheerful at having egged Dave to go on justifying and encouraging for so long—which was one of the few ways he knew of getting him to talk.

'If we make a living wage,' Donnie put in, 'what does it matter?'

Dave steered them back to work: ''Ark at 'im—bin listening to the conservatives. Thinks he's got a right to a living wage. Come on, let's stop boggering around, and get cracking.' At which they alighted onto the pavement, took up their particular sacks, and spread in three directions into rainshot streets.

Such free-lance fending had sharpened Donnie's powers of reconnaissance. Each backyard—from dustbin to lavatory, clothes-line to wooden palings—was assessed for articles of value: a thrown-out bicycle, a zinc bathtub on the wall, a sack-covered mangle waiting for washday. He noticed blinds down for a funeral, milk bottles on doorsteps and, on entering a street or terrace, immediately looked for what chimney-stacks sent out no smoke in this land of mineral plenty. Not, of course, that he would walk off with anything that didn't belong to him—his thieving days had ended during the war, when to go on living demanded a definite long spate of thieving —but to remove some backyard eyesore of mildewed pram or stack of scrap copper or ripped up firegrate would be a favour he couldn't be bad tempered enough to deny anyone. Hadn't a woman pleaded with them only the other week to shift stuff they knew they wouldn't get five bob for?

His roped-together mackintosh was darkened by rain. The wind rose, couldn't make up its mind which way to scatter the floods. He'd collected nothing. Locusts and desert, he thought. Every crumb scratched and scraped—and saw himself in the same mind maybe as those poor enormous animals in pre-historic times come to the end of their tether because the sun had dried up the earth—which was better than this wet.

He knocked at a back door and, after a prolonged rattling of bolts and latches it was pulled violently inwards, irritation sounding even in the squeak of its hinges. A tall, thin, middle-aged collier stood there, still in his shirt-sleeves from the night shift. His deep grey eyes flashed:

'What do yo' want?'

Donnie usually spoke first, making his request against a blank stare. But this time he was stopped dead by abrupt rage in the collier's face as if, should it turn out he had been dragged from his breakfast for nothing, he would swing the hand from behind and wield a pick over Donnie's head, ready to bring down a well-aimed prostrating blow.

'Any old rags, mate?'

The collier's scarred features took time off to consider. Then: 'Ar,' he bawled, 'Tek me'—and slammed the door at his face.

He wondered whether his brothers were having better luck. A whippet, entombed in some distant kennel, howled dismally at the general condition of the rheumatic world. Rain belted down, yet the sun shone in Donnie's brain of daydream and optimism, illuminating the sudden find of lead-rolls outside some half-built church he would never pray in, laughing like mad with his brothers as they set upon the gold-find with axe and crowbar, stuffing sack after sack which would weigh on their shoulderbones till they felt sick with lugging it to the lorry. A raindrop running down to his ear caused him to scrub away the itch of it. He missed half a dozen houses due to his daydream. The collier's rebuff seemed so comic that he thought to tell it later to his brothers for a laugh.

He knocked at another door, and a woman opened it, a cherubic tow-headed kid making an aeroplane out of the collection leaflet. She held an old brass kettle: 'If you've come for scrap, you can tek this, my lad.'

'How much do you want for it?' he said, thinking it better than nothing.

'Nay, lad, I'll tek nowt from thee, seeing as tha's had such a lot to put up with in the war, while many a one was staying at home.'

He looked modestly into the kitchen beyond. 'That's the way it is.'

'It's a bleddy shame they don't look after you better when you've been all them miles away fighting for 'em, it is and all.'

'Well,' Donnie said, 'as long as they fill their own pockets. I was in a Jap prison camp seven years. I've still got scars all over me, and one of my lungs is gone. I don't like to think about it. There's many a night I wake up all of a groan and sweat. And what did we get when we come back? Twenty-six bob a week. No good to a living soul. But I've got eleven kids now, so I suppose I'm good for something.' He stuffed the kettle into his sack, left his thanks as the door closed. He heard her going through the parlour muttering loudly to the un-comprehending kid: 'Seven years! Poor bogger. Seven—that's funny, though.'

At the end of the street stood a red-bricked chapel, a body-snatcher guarded by railings and fronted by wide steps leading to the principal door. It was a chapel no longer, but a get-together of shabby drill-hall and dead-beat billiard saloon. Donnie found a nub-end pinned under the crossband of his cigarette case. Maybe they're clearing the place out, he thought, for it looked as if it were about to fall flat on its face. He pushed open a side gate and walked up the entry. The back-yard hadn't seen sunshine since its walls were built. Windows were wooden-barred and barbed-wire. Broken bottles spiking the top bricks turned it into a well-defended backyard of the house of God. Donnie noticed a row of dustbins, each caved-in or holed, which several experienced kicks showed to be empty. He grunted at the dampness, a dispiriting waterlogged atmosphere more tied to an outlaw's heart than any other smell and feeling.

He glanced back for a last check-up. Under an awning of corrugated tin stood a canvas kitbag tied at the neck. He went over and, giving it an immediate kick, expected the unresistant cave-in of cardboard and paper, but was not sur-prised (already suspecting that it looked too good for any old rubbish) when his boot hit against some kind of metal. He thumped it for being so puzzling, closed his fingers over corners of whatever was inside, Undo the string, you silly bogger, and have a look—an irritating and unrewarding job, for his fingernails broke at the first try. He stood back a moment: the cord was knotted and double-knotted, had shrunk and solidified in the damp air.

He was bemused, at what a kitbag meant to many but had never meant to him. Gunner Donnie Hodson—you didn't keep your kitbag long: came on leave one day and never went back—stayed by the fireside in a long paralysis of fear and rage, smoking what fags you could cadge until your mother chucked you out and told you to get some money or clamb. Them was funny times. One day he was at the kitchen table when knocks—back and front—sounded from the wide-awake street. He was hungry for his tea, holding a sharp knife and not knowing whether to cut his throat or a slice of bread. His mother did what was needed of her. Donnie ran up to the attic, coolly setting the skylight down when once on the roof. And there he was, hanging out on the slates like Monday washing, under the summer sky and counting German planes that slid over low and let rip with machine-guns. Shellbursts like dirty wool seemed to be exploding not many feet from his head. The sirens were moaning like a runover cat, and it was hard to imagine anyone in his right mind out on the roof— so the coppers must have thought. But Donnie wasn't in anybody's mind except his own, which turned out to be right enough, and his instinct told him one sure thing, that it was better to risk a bullet from German planes than go back through that skylight and get parcelled off to the army again. 'What did mam do with them two full cups of tea she'd just poured? Did she sling 'em in the sink before the coppers could see 'em?'—were his sole speculations as shrapnel (from AA shells he would have been firing had he not been where he was) zipped viciously by like petrified dead sparrows onto the slates, breaking some, others ricochetting, one piercing the skylight window that finally stopped the coppers' courage from thinking he was out there.

Looking back on this one uncomfortable glory of his life,

he couldn't help but laugh. Nothing from the past was sad, no matter how awful it might have been at the time. Only the present was classifiable into good or putrid, but every incident that he could remember was laughable for the simple reason that it was past, and that he had survived it without mortal damage. While Donnie was sitting on the rooftop with shrapnel and bullets pissing all around, his mother was being questioned by coppers and redcaps, unable to speak out where he was, yet wanting to in order to get him off that dangerous roof.

They got him in the end, cornered as a rat by bigger rats in a cul-de-sac one dark night, a suitcase of plundered whisky at his feet. Dave had got away, rattled his longer legs among streets at different angles to Donnie's, until dark distance drew him into a maw of safety. Donnie was pounced on by a couple of stalwart Specials and manhandled to the police station: 'We're helping our country'—bump—'and trying to do our bit,'—bump—'but you blokes are worse than the bloody Germans'—bump-thud. 'You want bleeding-well exterminating, then maybe we could get this war finished'—crash. No bail (the black eyes and cuts had disappeared by quartersessions time). Twenty-two cases to be taken into consideration, sir. Three years, then. And let that be a lesson to you. Yes, sir. Thank you, sir.

That was the only way to get the war over. Go and fight, they had said. What for? Show me what I've got to fight for, and then I'll go. You can't though, can you? There's nobody in this bloody country can show me that. 'You're a pacifist,' Dave dinned into him. 'Like me. See?' It was still the middle of the war when they let him out of jail and turned him over to the redcaps, so he hopped it a second time, and uniform number two burst into paraffin-flame from the bedroom grate.

In 1945 the redcaps collared him for the final bout, made him pay for having kept out of the war as successfully as they had by declaring on him a private and spiteful war of their own. Even that terrible time was laughable. He had wakened up one fine day to find himself between the clean sheets of heaven. 'A mental home,' the man in the next bed grinned.

Marvellous. No more bread-and-water, cells, packdrill, kick. and punches and buckets of freezing pond-scum splashing against thin denims. You had to laugh, at what men who should have been your own mates in factory or on building site did to you. You just couldn't help laughing, though you could bet that some bastards had put them up to it as well. Such a grin gave you toothache on the lips. It was funny, too funny even to tell anyone about, and so Donnie had a reputation for being soft, almost daft and, unlike his brothers, slow in ways of self-preservation. He was also reluctant with his speech, dense it was said, often unable to make his opinions fit the subject under discussion, or make them influence it when they did. His family and friends began to think that such attitudes had been there from birth, to be pointed out and taken advantage of.

The rain was a mere drizzle, easier to accept and fight, and he shook himself to regard the actual physical bulk of the kitbag. This one stored rubbish—a useful purpose to what most carried. He searched for another cigarette, but found none. 'I'll ask Dave to lend me one when I get back. I'd better start moving, or they'll wonder where I've got to.'

He pulled the bag forward, held it from the ground by unyielding strings. It weighed heavy and, replacing it, a piece of cardboard finished its journey and slid onto the stones behind. Torn from a shoebox and crayoned on the white surface, the words he held up were: TO BE COLLECTED.

His heart bumped. By who else but him? A find, it looked like. Who'd have thought it in all this drenching rain? It was meant for the scrapman to pick up and relieve whoever had left it of an unwanted rubbish-burden. It felt like old metal against his boot, a mixture of bits and bobs no doubt, that would need sorting but hadn't been considered valuable enough to sell. It was no use sorting it now: he pictured his brothers doing that like vultures later, cursing him, he shouldn't wonder, because the stuff—after his dreams of a unique find—wasn't worth much after all. Still, it was marvellous to get something. He spat on both palms and honed them well, lifted the bag onto his broad shoulders and lugged it out into the street, a miracle that such a light heart supported it.

Most of their time back at the lorry had been spent cursing Donnie—'The dilat'ry bastard'—for dawdling, when from their vantage point of the high cab they saw him staggering along the street with what looked like a treasure of a load. Old rags didn't weigh that much, for Donnie was a carthorse, a man of iron never known to flinch or tire under the most back-breaking weights. So what could it be and where had he clicked to be shouldering such heavy responsibility?

'Trust old mental to get all the luck,' Bert said. A grateful feeling lurked somewhere behind his scowl, though he could only show it by feeling envious. 'We didn't even get a bleddy claprag between us. Where did you find it?' he bawled.

'From a church.'

The metal was all sharp elbows, dug corner after merciless corner into the muscle of Donnie's shoulders. The pressure had now passed aching point, become pain—fiery and unbearable. At Bert's abrupt question, though only a few yards from the lorry, he let the sack roll over his head and crash logwise onto the wet pavement. It pulled his new cap off: 'Can't you bleddy-well wait till I get to the lorry?' he shouted angrily at Bert. Dave was helping him to carry it there.

Bert hung back, opening and closing the blade of his jack-knife. The crash sounded tinny, like kids toys hammered together to take up less room—but Donnie wouldn't know the difference. Old wool-nut thought all metal a miracle of gold and silver, and only leapt into life at the noise it made. Which perhaps was a good thing for a bloke on this job, for look how he'd toted that sack from God knew where. Bert slid to the pavement when all work was done, snapping strings with his razorsharp knifeblade.

'Steady-on,' Donnie cried. 'Give me a chance to get the bleddy thing down. You'll slice my finger off if you aren't careful.' He stood back, sullen while they ravaged his prize. Bert started to unthread the cord through each eye-hole, but was beaten to it by nimble, systematic Dave. All three fixed their eyes on it at the same time.

Dave held it as he must at some time have been taught to during his various brief stays with the army: left hand under the barrel a little behind the spout, arm out at a sufficient angle to give rest to the magazine—which he instinctively slotted on; right hand at the trigger; and skeleton-butt under his arm. Then it swivelled downwards, mouth pouting to the pavement.

'Christ!' he said, all breath shocked from him. Bert balanced a slender tin casing of magazine on his palm. It was full of bullets. 'What sort of a chapel did you say you got it from?' He was amused, as much at Dave's tight-set face seeing prison and death and all the discomforts that oscillated between for possessing such a thing, as at the sight of the Sten machine-gun he unwillingly toted. Donnie was the least surprised or perturbed, still thought of it as scrap, guns and magazines to be sledge-hammered into solid unrecognizable slabs and flogged at the junkyard. Nobody would know. It had been done before; and they might be as much as a quid each to the good.

Dave turned on him: 'You *barmy* bleeder. You crazy bastard. Bringing things like this!'

Maybe he was putting on a rare joke, though the pained face made Donnie suspect him in earnest. 'What do you mean? What are you calling me like that for?'

A woman, carrierbags hooked to each hand, came around the corner from the main road. Dave rammed the gun under cover and they talked about last night's film. 'I suppose you're going to tell me you found 'em in a dustbin next?' he demanded when she had passed.

'They was near a dustbin,' Donnie explained, hurt at such ingratitude. 'A card was on top of the bag saying: TO BE COLLECTED. Somebody meant it for us, I'm dead sure o' that. It's government surplus maybe, that's all.'

Dave's anguished face showed he was nowhere convinced. He set the bag down a yard from himself: 'Carry 'em up the street again.'

'Not me. Yo' can do it if you like.'

'We'll get ten years each in bleeding jail if you don't.'

Donnie climbed into the cab and slammed the door on himself. 'That's the bleddy thanks I get for struggling all that way with it.'

'He might get nicked taking 'em back,' Bert said. 'We'd better dump 'em on the lorry and get shot on 'em when we come to a lonely place.'

The whole day boggered, Dave plainly saw. Would you believe it? That was the worst o' working with batchy bleeders like Donnie. His narrowed eyes, grizzled hair and creased forehead gave an impression of forcefulness that would never break. 'It's looney,' he said, yet saw reason in Bert's advice. He slung the sack on the lorry-back. 'All right, Bert'— giving unrepentant Donnie a black look—'let's get cracking out of here. We'll drop 'em in a reservoir somewhere.'

Bert drove to the main road as if to go quietly from the pitch of their crime, filtered through the traffic of Hilltop and descended into the valley, eager to put distance between them and Eastwood. 'I expect it's only scrap though, you know.'

'Course it is'—a desperate note in Donnie's voice—'They wouldn't 'ave put it there if it worn't. I don't know. All this bother over a few bits o' junk.'

'You mental bastard,' Dave cried. 'You think it's scrap— with ammunition? It might have been army surplus but we worn't supposed to tek it. Anybody with a bit o' sense would have known it. I expect you thought they put it there for us, specially? "Perhaps somebody'll want to start a revolution," I suppose you thought they said. "Or maybe somebody'll want to do a bit o' target practice at the rent man, or knock off the odd copper or two?" Christ!' He banged his fist against the lorry door, emphasizing a decision that needed no democratic majority to force it through: 'We'll get rid of it somewhere past Ripley, then beat it back to Nottingham. I only hope nobody gets onto us about it, that's all. If they do, I'll brain you. You might want to get away from your ten kids for a few years, but I don't.'

'It'd be better if we could sell it though,' Bert said. 'I know an IRA bloke who'd give his right arm for stuff like this.

Happen we could dump it somewhere, and then let him know where it is, at a price.'

Fields, hedged by mounds of stone, rose from either side of the road. Towns were far behind. Dave turned to his brother: 'Look, nut, if you think I'm going to get twenty years, you're wrong.' His hand went to the door: 'I'm getting out.'

'I was only joking,' Bert said, though slowing down in case Dave really wanted to get out. But he pulled the door to and they drove on in silence, three factions as much as three brothers.

Beyond Ambergate lay tranquil countryside, low cloud and rainmist on purple inhospitable hills around the Matlocks. The road contoured into another valley, and no one spoke. Such wild land kept words penned in. Donnie's normal face was one of open good-humoured speculation as to whether the day would yield fair loads and a living wage, but his triumphant find at the chapel ('It couldn't have been a chapel,' he told himself now) gave it a self-importance that his brothers would not acknowledge; at which his face gave way to gloom, like some forlorn box-headed terrier that retrieves a succulent rabbit for its poaching master but feels it change into a rat while the smile of achievement awkwardly persists.

Rain hung, a carbide sheet of blue above grey-green rolling hills around. Trees were bowed down by the weight of water, bare twigs shining silver with it, the soaked smell of the green and soily earth more extreme and frightening than the rancid stink of protective streets. Hopeful Donnie assumed that every wayside house was a missed opportunity of a brass bedstead or heap of iron and lead. But Dave sat immersed in the webbed roads of his map, and Bert's eyes showed only a flat concern for his firm motionful steering along the highway.

Dave grunted them into a by-road and Bert silently obeyed, putting the lorry at grinding first gear for a steep incline. The high-roaring life of the engine plunged Donnie's memory back to another faraway lorry that, in the depths of a smoke-screen, increased speed regardless of what might be in its way.

He was going on foot through a paraffin midnight, each quiet step betrayed by a choking cough, delayed by a case bulging with silk stockings snaffled from a shop hidden within the bull's-eye of a few dozen shrouded streets.

On the boulevard a woman screamed, and Donnie jumped (the first time afraid that evening) thinking she was under its double wheels. He was close enough to touch her. 'Where are you, duck?' he called, as the unheeding vehicle thundered away. 'Are you all right?'

The voice that answered sounded young and sweet, even behind such swearing laid on at the unthinking driver: 'The bleddy swine might a killed me.'

'Tek my arm,' Donnie said. 'I'll see you 'ome. Did you miss your last bus?'

'Aye,' she answered, quick off the mark, 'I did.'

'What a shame,' Donnie said, leading her along, and thinking that most likely some chap had ditched the poor gel.

Her name was Dora and, talking readily, they made a harmless couple passing the copper propping up the labour-exchange in the artificial fog. They went home to Donnie's, and slept a sinful sweet kip together. From his attache-case Dora thought he was a nice young man, a commercial traveller perhaps (which he was but not in the way she thought) and fairly well-off when he opened the case in the morning and gave her a dozen pairs of fully-fashioned stockings; and Donnie, when they decided that same day to live together ('I've got a house in Cuckney Terrace just down the road,' she told him) deduced her to be living alone because her husband was in the Forces. Both, thinking they were on to a good thing, were disappointed. Dora found soon enough that Donnie was on the run and thieving for a living; and Donnie discovered even sooner that Dora already had four children in the house (floors and faces well-scrubbed though to receive him) and that she was separated from her husband because he was in jail. Such disappointments cancelled out, and they were happy together. Donnie stole hard to keep her and the kids, liked being the master of his house and having something to go steady for. Dora loved him and bred well so that there were three more kids by Victory Day. 'We'll buy the silly bleeder a dartboard, or a game of ludo,' Dave said. 'He thinks there ain't owt else to do in the world but that.'

'You'd do better to whitewash his cellar out and knock a few bunks together,' Bert answered. 'If it worn't already full up.'

One of the children could not have been Donnie's, not well enough synchronized with his spells in prison, but he accepted it just the same. This, he found, lowered him still further in the eyes of his brothers: 'She's done it on him, the poor bogger. If she was my woman I'd paste her from one end of Hyson Road to the other,' he heard Bert say once when he came in from the bookie's because he'd lost his money sooner than intended. 'I shouldn't be a bit surprised if none o' them kids are 'is,' his mother was saying. 'She's an old bag, and nowt else,' Dave said sternly as Donnie came in through the scullery. 'How else could she have lived, though, while he was in clink?' was the final verdict.

Riding along with a load of hot guns, all silent because they'd share a life sentence if caught, Donnie felt they were ripping away his credit for what could be a profitable find. His grievance came from the memory of his desperate yet strangely happy years during the war, and of what he had overheard after his bad luck on the horses which only now did he relate to himself—and so long ago, he thought, beaming his mortally injured sight on the set visages of Dave and Bert.

A sun blade made the road shine like a roll of liquorice. Clouds moved above wooded spurs and crags of the lonely Pennines whither Dave had guided them by constant reference to his magic map. 'They have wicked weather out here,' he said. 'Only a month ago the snow nearly covered the telegraph poles. I'd rather be in streets.' It was a long time since they passed a house, and none were now in sight. The woods seemed dead and February bare, yet when Bert stopped the lorry under a hill bushes showed spring buds like the green tips of novelty matchsticks.

They got down, stamped their feet morosely against wind and the smell of open country beating up their limbs; it felt clean and agreeable to the stale stink of cab and backyards. Dave led them over a five-barred gate and down a bank. Bert carried the kitbag to a large pool of stagnant water, hurled a stone towards the middle that landed with a healthy penetrating sound: gluck! 'It's deep. Be good enough to swim in, if it worn't so cold.'

Dave, slashing the bag with a penknife, looked at Donnie as if he would slash him next: 'All we want now is for a copper to come by. Think of the time and petrol we've lost on this stunt.'

Shirtsleeves rolled up, Bert rubbed the beneficial ointment of wind into his white heavily veined skin. 'It's like a holiday. Leave Donnie be,' he said. 'We know how you feel by now.'

Donnie stood by the rising ground, feeling the injustice of their so-called democracy. His great effort of the rain-soddened morning had come to this!—slung into deep and muddy water, sunk out of sight when they had stood to make a fiver each— which he for one could do with, Dora being pregnant and soon to leave for the hospital. He'd often thought how this ragman job was too low paid, having such a mob of kids to look after, but the family allowance helped, and it was better than working for a gaffer no matter how low the money. He had been the one brother reluctant to part with his hundred pounds, giving in eventually because without it there'd be no business—something they had willingly forgotten. And now they'd got the sort of find often imagined with glowing eyes and pints suspended they were chucking it away, just like that. 'Come on,' Dave cried. 'Give a hand to get rid o' this stuff.'

Donnie couldn't move. 'I'm for keeping it. What about yo', our Bert?'

'I'm snatched,' Bert said, struggling back into his coat. He turned to Donnie: 'I don't know. Honest to God, I don't.'

Dave picked out the top Sten gun. 'I do. It's got to be slung away. If it ain't I'm not getting in that lorry again. I'd rather walk back to Nottingham.' His words burned with righteousness, and of all three he had the clearest ideas of right and wrong (though he didn't always abide by them), which made him a hard man to argue with. At election times Donnie never voted; Bert sometimes dragged himself between one pint and the next; Dave always did, being at heart a simple political man and swearing at others whom he suspected of not having bothered. With him an idea once expressed stuck until a new one took its place, causing the old one to fuse with the hard core of his personality.

Bert turned to Donnie: 'I reckon we'd better sink 'em. They aren't any good to us. Too risky to keep, as well'—an opinion sending Dave into action before Donnie tried once more to swing the vote. The first gun sailed to the middle of the water. It sank. Another followed. Bert joined in, threw a gun and tailed it with a hollow magazine.

Donnie strolled casually over and picked out a gun, as if to help, then sorted through rusting magazines until he reached one that was loaded. He clipped it onto his gun, the sound hidden by resplendent waterspouts caused by the hard work of his brothers. 'This is what they should a done in the war,' Dave said.

'I thought that was what yo' did,' Bert laughed.

'I mean everybody though.'

'Maybe they will in the next one.'

'There wain't be a next one, or time to do this if there is'— Dave spun the last weapon as high as it would go, the two of them drawing their heads back—seeing bordering rocks, treetops and a gulf of cloud—to follow the upward and downward flight. 'A bull's-eye,' Bert shouted, blinking at its impact. 'Chock in the middle.'

Dave gave in to a rare bout of self-praise. 'I can't help it if I'm a crackshot!'

A savage, sharp explosion burst through the air, a needling crack of white fire directly connected with the chip that flew from the moss-covered rock a bare yard from Bert's foot. The shot itinerated every crevice-point of the hills, came back again and again, each time with diminishing vigour.

The sight of Donnie holding the machine-gun, as if he had been a professional guerilla all his life, sent a pain through Dave's feet that seemed to come from the soil he stood on, fastening him to earth and shrubs like a charge of electricity high enough to cause a rheumatic pain but not to sling him a dozen yards away. He was afraid to move, to try and rid himself of it in case it would increase—or for fear a bullet from Donnie's gun would strike him all unbeknowing—smack in the guts. He stared at the apparition of his brother, was startled by Bert calling: 'Drop it, Donnie, you daft sod. Come on, nark it. You'll do some damage if you aren't careful.'

'That's right,' Dave said, and to Bert: 'You should a kept your bloody eye on him.' The derogatory tone, stabbing through to Donnie's incensed brain, brought forth a further terrifying shot. Dave and Bert scampered towards different boulders beyond the pool. 'Why don't you mind what you're saying?' Bert hissed across to Dave. Then in a commanding yet considerate tone: 'Donnie, put that bleeding gun down. I'll get mad in a minute.'

Donnie's fallen cap lay at the edge of the pool, half in and half out of the water like a turtle emerging for a breath of air. His face was rigid, all lines and muscles clamped into place by the grip of his teeth. His hair blew in the wind. 'You bastards'—a tearful implacable roar—'you rotten lousy bastards.'

'What's bitin' you?' Bert shouted. 'What 'ave we done to you?'

'I'll kill you both,' he responded loudly, his brain shut hard against the wind, and all their talk. 'You've 'ad it your own way too long. I'll show you whether I'm kidding or not. That's what Dora's allus telling me, that you put on me. Only I ain't believed her up to now.'

'Pack your game up,' Dave said reasonably, 'and let's get cracking. We've lost enough time as it is.'

'Chuck that gun in the water,' Bert ordered. 'Or I'll get mad, our Donnie.' The sun came out and, standing between them, gave Bert confidence to move nearer Donnie. He knelt at the kitbag to fold it: 'We'd better tek this with us and burn it. We don't want anybody to find it.'

'I suppose not,' Dave winked.

'You bastards,' Donnie said. 'You think you're the bosses

and can get away with everything.' His eyes were set on them, unmoving, as hard as the spout of the ever-pointing gun. 'You should a kept them Stens and not thrown 'em away. You'll be sorry you wasted 'em like that one day.'

'I told you it was dangerous,' Dave said. 'Our Bert said so as well. You don't want to go to clink for ten years, do you? I don't, anyway, I know that much. What would Dora do if you got sent down? Eh?'

Donnie pressed a foot forward. 'I don't give a fuck for owt now. I'll do you both in.'

'Put it away,' Dave shouted. 'You cranky sod.'

Bert eyed him coolly: 'If you do owt daft, you'll swing.'

'I don't care.'

'You will. Wain't he, Dave?'—nonchalantly.

'Not much he wain't. He'll get my fist as well when I catch hold of him.'

Bert was nearer now, pushing the spacious kitbag over his boots in a kneeling-down position and easing his feet forward while he talked: 'I know a bloke in the army had his arm shot off, only by accident, but the bloke who done it got ten years. I reckon he deserved it though: an arm's an arm, and a pension's no good to anybody. I don't like guns being pointed at me our Donnie, so you'd better drop it; it brings my cough back, and I feel bad for days then. I get laid-up and earn no dough, so stop it.'

'You never listen to what I say,' Donnie complained, crashing in on Bert's monologue. 'You think I'm daft. Two on to one. That's how it is all the time. I've only got to say: "Let's do this," and you two rotten bastards allus vote it down. But my share in this lorry's the same as yourn, you know. You forget that, you do an' all.'

'I never say it ain't,' Bert reassured him. 'You know I don't' —forward again, still closer. Dave, watching, wondered how it was going to end—'I'm allus on your side, but you forget that as soon as I see fit to vote with Dave once in a while. Don't he, Dave?'

'That's what I tell him.'

'You remember that time you wanted to tek Dora and the

kids on an outing to Gunthorpe, and Dave said we couldn't afford the time, and that we should collect some stuff from Derby instead? I voted with you then. So you won, and all your tribe had a smashing day by the Trent.'

Dave backed him up: 'Course they did. He's a mad-head though, wain't listen to anybody.'

He was deeply hurt, accused of disloyalty. 'Yes I do,' was all he could think of.

'No you don't. If you do, put that gun down and prove it. You've already made enough noise to bring all the coppers of Derby onto us, and I don't want to see yo' nor any on us copped. Come on, I'm clambed to death. Aren't yo', Bert?'

Dave imagined a reasonable tone would now creep into their discussion, then: 'I'm going to count seven,' Donnie said slowly, 'and when I've counted seven I'm going to empty this magazine into the pair of you. Then we'll see who's got a vote and who ain't. One, two, three'—loud like bullets already flying, a supercharged tone of voice he had often heard ordering him about, but had never been able to use himself.

Bert broke in. 'Donnie, you rat'—and moved closer, covered by his ruse of the kitbag. Dave stood, graven.

'Four, five'—slow and definite, each echo overriding Bert's plea, moving the gunspout now in a circular pointing motion that, though not making for accuracy, gave fate chance to operate and seemed more menacing. 'Donnie, chuck it,' Dave yelled. 'You can have the bleeding lorry, but drop that gun.' Bert had stopped moving, was fastened by Donnie's eyes.

'Six, seven!'

Nothing happened. 'Who are you kidding?' Bert said, standing up.

Donnie grinned. 'You thought I meant it, didn't you? Well I do. But if you think I'm going to do it when you expect it though, you're both bleddy-well wrong.' Bert's senses were fixed hard between guile and humour, and he said with a smile: 'Drop that rod, and I'll strip stark naked and swim in to get them guns out, one at a time—then we'll flog 'em to the IRA. Eh? What do you think o' that, then?'

It made no impression against Donnie's maniacal stare. Without warning, his arms lifted for the aim.

Bert fell to the ground, flattened like a spread-out frog. Dave followed, keeling over like a post, low-current electricity of fear moving like a threat through his limbs. Donnie's arms spun like propellers working in competition, and after several illogical movements both gun and magazine somehow parted and leapt free of his swinging arms, falling into the water. On lifting their heads—a broad margin of some seconds after the splash—they saw Donnie widely grinning.

'Oh you should a seen yer! Christ, you should a seen yer! Frightened to death, the pair of you. What a treat! Never in all my born days . . .'

They ran at him, wild for vengeance, and before they reached him Donnie knew it was no use making out it had been a joke. Gaiety withered on his face.

'You swine,' Dave screamed, gripping his waist and dragging him down. He had wanted to smash Donnie's life out, had promised himself the marvellous vicious treat of it while petrified by the Sten in such crazy hands—but a relatively harmless grip was all he could give now that the time had come. Bert found Donnie's head from out of the scuffle, and thumped him between the eyes in a business-like way, hard. 'You cranky bastard, doing a thing like that.'

In spite of smoke-stacks and colliery headstocks the distant landscape was clear: sun out to stay and clouds lingering only to the cold watery north. Bert manoeuvred the lorry like a madman, light hearted now that their incriminating load had been cast off. The lorry, it seemed, was a sort of zip mechanism causing the road to fasten-off the hills behind them as they descended. Dave sang snatches of song they had beaten out together in last Saturday's pub, the map crushed and stained under his muddy boots. Donnie sat between them, smiling, his face dirty, hand at last taken from the swollen eye sustained in the final settlement at the pool. Dave put an arm around his shoulders, pulled him close, hugged him: 'Old barmy sod. Old madhead'—yet with a certain deference that Donnie was too happy, and Bert too careful at the corner before Ripley, and Dave too close to it, to notice.

Donnie pulled away. 'Less of the barmy,' he threatened, as if still holding the Sten.

'Hark at him,' Dave sang back. 'Scarface. Al Capone. It's a good job we got rid o' them guns, or he'd a bin down at Barclays tomorrow asking for a loan.'

'Bogger off,' Donnie retaliated, though laughing with them at such a Robin Hood picture and grateful that it saved him feeling foolish for having stuck them up. 'I wouldn't do owt as daft as to rob a bank.' Here was a story they could talk and laugh about for ever among themselves, without being able to tell it to another and so mock Donnie with.

'Well, I don't know about that,' Dave said. 'In a way maybe we should a kept one o' them guns. If there's a war and they come to call us up we could take to the hills with it. Mow down a few Civil Defence bastards on the way. All three on us, wi' the lorry. We'd never get caught.'

Donnie was indignant. 'Now hark at who's talking. Christ! That's what I was trying to tell you back there. It's too bleddy late now.'

Dave's imagination drew back, having touched on some too open wound. He was the calm and thoughtful leader once more. 'Forget it. I'm only kidding.'

'Perhaps we should 'ave though,' Bert said, feeling for the crumpled kitbag between his legs, aiming punches that swerved the lorry from one side of the house-lined street to the other. 'We could a kept two or three. Donnie was right.'

'No he worn't,' Dave said, but quietly. 'And I'm telling the pair of you—that you don't know owt about no guns— that you've never seen any. Forget 'em, see?'

'They'll never find 'em,' Bert said.

'What a bloody time we 'ad though,' Dave laughed, nudging Donnie.

'I wonder if Dora's had her kid yet?' Bert asked, spitting out of the window. 'I can see owd Donnie ending up better off than any on us. He'll be sitting back like a sheik while his twenty kids bring their wage packets back from the factory every week.'

'It's not due for a day or two,' was all Donnie said. Drab windswept houses funnelled them up the hill, and dinner could be detected journeying from gas-ovens to tables of waiting children home from school. 'It's only one o'clock,' Bert said, stopping at the market place, 'but I feel as if a week's gone by since this morning.'

'Shall we eat here, or in Heanor?' Dave wanted to know. Smells from a snackbar drifted over the cobbles as a bus conductor opened the door and stood fastening his silver-buttoned coat over a just-fed belly.

'Here,' Bert opted, 'I'm clambed.'

'I reckon we should go to Heanor,' Donnie said. 'It ain't far off.' Bert said they could eat just as well where they were, so Donnie turned to Dave: 'What about yo'? At that place in Heanor you can get a big plate o' stuff for a couple o' bob.'

Bert pulled the door shut. 'Let's make our bleddy minds up.' Cigarettes were lit to relieve the strained atmosphere of voting. Fingers drummed hard on the drumsounding door. Dave's long face made up its mind, yet no sign was showed of a decision: 'Heanor.'

Even on the second syllable Bert had given in and pulled out the choke, and they were rolling down the hills again towards Eastwood. Once a majority vote was reached it became a unanimous decision. A hard wind drove tension clear of the cab. 'I forgot to tell you,' Donnie said. 'It was a scream.' He laughed until Dave told him to get on with it then. 'Well, I went to this house at Eastwood, before I found the guns, and a collier comes to the door, a great big bastard still in his helmet and pit-muck, his trousers patched and his vest in tatters. "What do *yo*' want?" he bawls out at me. I thought he was going to smash me with the pick he's got in his hand. So I says: "Got any old rags, mate?" And he looks at me for half a minute, then says, "Ar, TEK ME!" and slams the door in my face.'

It was the best joke in years: three crimson faces choking behind the windscreen of the descending lorry. Bert pulled into the side of the road and switched off, tears flowing from all but Donnie, who knew it was a good story, but wasn't paralysed by it. When the lorry started again he felt happy—in spite of the half-soaked cap (rescued at the last minute from the pool) whose damp side ate through to his hair—singing to himself because Dora might have another boy. He still didn't know why he'd insisted that they eat in Heanor because, all said and done, it didn't matter to him where they ate, as long as he was able to fill his aching guts with something.

THE GOOD WOMEN

I am in a police cell, stretched full length on the floor and packed in with eleven others. Nobody talks. The last chocolate has been shared and we are all dead beat, trying to sleep in the dull stupefying parsimonious emanation called light which comes from the ceiling. I could have been in bed, snug and warm and knocked out by the refuelling powers of rest, but I had refused bail and so been thrown into the nick. As far as any of us knew we'd get two months in the morning, so maybe to help me realize what it meant I counted on my fingers the immediate members of my family who had been inside, and got as far as nine. Well, whether or not it turned out to be my first time, I had a good idea that it wouldn't be the last.

In Trafalgar Square the cops had moved in on us at twelve-thirty. To me anyway it was unexpected, for I'd imagined they'd just leave us to get fed-up and lose patience, disperse in the luminous realism of dawn light. Not that any of us would have, forming a hard core that would only shift when the coppers did labouring work and picked us bodily up. I was talking to Doris, when suddenly she went flying one way, and I the other.

I was dragged towards the police buses at the barrier, thinking: 'This isn't the way. I should be on my feet using my strength.' I remembered how a Nottingham pal of mine some weeks ago had been stopped for driving a lorry without a rear light. My pal hadn't known about it, but the cop was going to book him anyway, so his long arm shot from the cab and the cop went flying against a wall, the noise of his impact hidden by a mad engine starting up with unaccustomed speed. 'That's the only way you'll ever get them to ban that bleeding bomb,' he said, while telling me about it in the pub.

I wish I could believe him. The coppers bundled inert bodies up the steps of the bus, but when my turn came to be lifted in I said: 'I'll walk into the bus'—and did so.

In the cell I can't get to sleep. My brain is active, and I feel good. My bones ache and I am cold, but my face burns and, strangely enough, I think of people I knew and know in Nottingham, who also don't want to kick the bucket for Berlin and the Germans, or for the English or the Americans or anybody, and who also don't want this threat of war hanging over them. They have lives to lead, and nothing will disturb their sublime preoccupation with it more than death or injury.

I distrust the past, but like the people in it, because those same people walk about me. These figures come to me out of the past, show themselves on the cell wall of my mind. They dominate the present also: vivid, large, common. Many of them are women, the good women, and though this story only concerns Liza Atkin, they attain the height of visions, strong faces that reinforce each other, that change more slowly than the immediate circumstances of their lives.

As a kid there were fathers, police, and women to fear and look out for—in no particular order, but simply according to tactics and situation. The women were more omnipresent than the former two, as when Alf Atkin and I went into backyards and, on lead-collecting forays at the age of ten, tried to steal the outside lead pipe of a lavatory by pushing a stick into it and levering it up and down until it snapped off. Then we would bolt—as some door clicked open for a woman to give chase.

One time however a couple of meaty fists held our fore-arms like a pair of pliers even before we had snapped off the lead, and the formidable Mrs. Griffin dragged us helpless to her back door like a spider who would eat us up. 'Caught you,' she said. 'You little rogues. Come on in, come on'—as if she'd sat at her back window for the last five years waiting for us like two flies to tip-toe up the yard and begin our work on the assumption that everyone was out or asleep. Her grey hair was done up in a bun and her face was round like a cat's, not unpleasant, but self-satisfied, mouth and jaw determined to hold us.

We were bundled into her warm kitchen, and her husband, standing with his back to the fire even though it was a summer's afternoon said, unnecessarily: 'You got 'em, did you?'— as if for years he'd been polishing his meat-grinder for just such a capture as well.

It was a spotless kitchen, I had time to notice, the grate black-leaded and the fender shining like high quality brass that would fetch a good bob or two from the scrapyard—I saw with my professional eye. The house had a homely, clean smell, of baking and stewed tea. There were bird plaques on the wall and pot dogs on the shelf, even a picture of sunset above the mantelpiece, giving an impression of ancient order impossible to break from. In any case, if I made a dash for it I wouldn't have got far because my pockets were sagging with lead already plundered, and I only hoped that Mrs. Griffin wouldn't notice this. Trying to hide it must have given me a shifty look.

Mr. Griffin turned on us. 'You bleddy young fools. You might as well sit down, because you're going to be here for a long time. Go on, sit down.'

We sat, silent. He was a grey haired ex-corporation gas-meter man. His wife put on her coat: 'I'll go and get the police, so look after 'em.' I wanted to ask her not to go for the cops because we hadn't really done any damage, but I was obstinate and couldn't bring myself to plead with her. Anyway, I thought she was only saying she was going for the police just to frighten us good and proper, and that she wouldn't really bother to go.

But ten minutes later she came in the house, followed by a tall peak-capped copper, and I thought: 'This is it. Three years in an approved school for six pennorth o' lead.'

The copper asked my name, and I thought of giving a false one, but didn't because Mrs. Griffin knew it anyway. Then he took Alf's name and address, and all the time I was waiting for him to say: 'All right. Tip your pockets out'—because I had ten pounds of lead piping just waiting to rip and burst its way out of mine. Then we'd have got five years instead of three, or I would, rather, because Alf had no lead on him. He wasn't wearing his jacket that day so mine were the only pockets. 'Is this all the lead you tried to pinch?' he asked.

He turned to the Griffins: 'We've had a lot of complaints lately about lead pipes being stole.'

'Yes,' Alf said to him.

'Yes,' I told him, hoping my heart would start again.

'All right,' he said, 'go on home. I'll be down later to see your parents. Then we'll know what to do with you. And don't do anything like this again.'

I tried to stop my heavy pockets knocking against the door post as we went out, and then to walk up the yard as if I didn't weight a feather in case our three captors still watched from the window. The sky was blue and hot, chimney-pots and roofs parching it up. I blinked, almost in tears with rage at Mrs. Griffin having fetched the coppers. It was against the law to do it. She'd got no right. And now we had to wait for the coppers to come that night and drag us screaming off to clink. Alf was already on probation, and said he'd get sent down this time. He supposed I would, as well.

'Not if I know it,' I said, not liking the idea of it at all. 'I'm going to do a bunk. Run off somewhere. I'm going to start walking. They wain't find me.' It was an empty street, September and school having already started, though Alf and I hadn't. Both our houses were empty, so we took a loaf from one and a packet of tea from the other, and with the tea in my pocket and the bread under Alf's arm we made our way by the factory and onto the Derby road.

My thoughts were set, determination fixed. I'd already left home for good, would never see my mother and father, brothers and sisters again. I already felt the freedom of the world fall onto my shoulders. Good and exhilarating one minute, it frightened me the next, and then became good again. I had no choice but to run away, because when the freedom felt too sad and heavy and maybe holding hardship and peril in store, my legs took over my mind and walked me forward, on and on and on, relieving me of all thought or decision as to whether or not I was doing the right thing and should go back.

Alf was surprised at what he had agreed to. Now that I seemed determined to keep walking until I reached Wales, he couldn't try to stop me without appearing to lack the courage for going on. He was a few months older and had been in the courts, so it wouldn't do to be thought yellow in front of me.

'I expect we'll be at Derby before it gets dark,' I said. 'Sooner, if we can cadge a lift on a lorry. God knows where we'll end up. P'raps even London.' Wasn't it Alf who, whenever we came out of the Saturday pictures, ruined it by telling me in his know-all way that the films we'd seen had been cut by half, and that London was the only place where you could see them with no good bits chopped out?

'London's a long way,' he ventured now. 'My legs are aching already.'

'Well, we ain't even done a mile yet.'

'Perhaps we ain't, but they're bleddy well aching just the same.' We came to the main road, and I stood by the bridge parapet throwing pieces of lead onto the track, lightening my pockets of what had been stolen before our capture at Ma Griffin's. 'I wain't get so puffed or sweat so much now,' I said.

Alf didn't like me jettisoning our hard-gained loot so recklessly: 'There was three bob's worth there,' he grumbled, 'at least.'

'I know. But I didn't want a copper to see us with it.' I'd admitted my fear, which gave him an opening for his. 'It ain't no use running away. We've only got one and a tanner between us. You need a lot of money to run away.'

'We'll pinch some more,' I said. 'Live like bandits. One of my cousins did.' I didn't add that he was now at an approved school, but the thought stuck like a poisoned dart in myself.

'That copper might not come back for us tonight,' Alf said. 'He might forget.'

'Some hopes,' I scoffed, already knowing that luck only

worked when unexpected, never came when beckoned by hope. White clouds began sneaking into the sky, and though it was only four by Lenton church clock the breeze suggested the fall of evening and the bleak night of what could turn into a cold September. It was pure, wide-open day at the moment, but a real chill came from nowhere or somewhere, and I saw how there would be no food and fire and roof once we had really set out on our travels, and I wondered whether it would be worth it to avoid maybe a fine and a few punches from the old man and the cops.

I threw the rest of the lead on a goods train passing underneath, and walked on, down the slope and towards the distant hills and woods of Bramcote, on which the sun swarmed to make them stand out clear and desirable. I whistled, happy as I went, lighter now that my pockets held only the packet of tea.

I was walking on my own. Alf stayed at the bridge: 'I'm not going.'

Lorries and buses, cars and bikes crippled along in both directions. I turned, thinking what a hard life it was when people couldn't make up their minds. 'Why?'

'Because it's going to rain,' he answered. This baffled me. I walked a few yards more, but he still didn't come. Suppose he knew more than I did, being on probation? Maybe it would rain, and perhaps the copper wouldn't bother to come back. In any case it wouldn't be such an adventure, running away alone. I'd started to wonder, and that was bad.

I took a last look at the sun and clouds, that made the country appear so much more comforting than streets and thieving and the certainty of a bash across the mug when I got back home to them. Woods and fields went on for ever, rolling and nudging each other by church spires and roadside and Wollaton Hall and orchards. It was green, green, luminous in one patch, as if it were green water, dark in others like scabs of jungle in which one might be able to share life with foxes and rabbits and civet cats.

'It's raining already,' Alf said. 'I felt a spot.'

I'd wanted to go on, away from everything I'd known in

the world until then, and I suppose that if I had kept on, with the sort of brigand ideas that were rattling about in my head, I'd have been locked up years sooner than getting charged for obstruction last night in Trafalgar Square. But more than Alf stopped me, a sense of something not yet being complete in my brain and heart.

I made a cup of tea in our house, and then we went to the pictures, staying in until twenty to eleven. When I came down our yard that night lights blazed from our back window showing that the whole family was at home.

I walked into a mountain of dusty sparks and went staggering back against the cupboard, hearing through the mist of half consciousness blunt admonitions from my father. In bed I saw what Mrs. Griffin must have said to that copper: 'I just want you to come back and take their names, to frighten 'em, nowt else.' I decided she wasn't so bad after all. I was glad also that Alf had stopped me running away, though at the same time and in the half dreams of approaching sleep I couldn't help thinking about the lit-up fields and woods, and regretting that going to sleep wasn't the same as finding my way among them for good and all.

It must have been a couple of years before this incident that I first saw Liza Atkin. It was a windy day, and the grudging sun of autumn polished a lucky chimney-pot here and there, made a slate roof look suddenly wet (though not warm) when it came out. It was so windy that even the oil and steel pong from the factory smelt fresh.

Turning the corner at the top of the street came a woman pushing a decrepit pram. Half hiding the pram, and balanced uneasily on it, was a large kitchen table with stumpy legs. The wind was erratic and vicious, as if filled with invisible fists determined to punch the table from the pram and hurl it where Liza had no intention of going. Yet she had foreseen this and, taking the place of sheet anchors, were two young boys of about my own age set on either side of the table to steady it. This was a hard job, causing them to pull and slide all over the cobbles, for their mother pushed the pram down the middle of the street, shunning the more protected areas of the house shadows.

As they drew near it was seen that Liza had no coat on, but an old brown jumper and a skirt. Her long dark hair blew around her lined, tanned face (she couldn't have been much more than thirty) and whenever it let her she smiled at every passer-by, saying: 'Hey, duck, what's it like living in this neighbourhood?'

'Not so good as where you come from,' some man said, hoping to find out from what part of Nottingham she had been turned. But she repeated her greeting and question to the next person, and though they learned much about her later, no one ever did discover where she came from on that windy day.

Her husband, carrying a small bath-tub and two carrier-bags, looked younger than Liza. He was a thin man with features so regular and thin that his moustache and watery blue eyes suggested he had been disappointed in not a few hopes and ambitions in his time, possibly through much of his own fault. Yet his expression did not seem terrified of the workless world around him, since he was wearing a good top coat, shining shoes, and a clean scarf.

I waited for a handcart or lorry to come with the rest of their household stuff, but what we'd seen was it, the lot, and for a long time they must have slept on straw and sackbags or, as I figured it, two on the table, one in the bath and one in the pram. In that way they needed only one warm room, but the house they went to had five, as well as an attic and kitchen. I also puzzled it out that during the day they ate off the table and washed in the bath.

As for the pram, Liza would sometimes push it down the street and over the bridge by Radford station, then onto the rubbish and rammel tips to fill it by dusk with wood, old rags or metal, in order to pull in a few bob a week and supplement the dole. Her husband—Ted—sat at home, except when he went to sign on and get his money, or look for a job he'd heard was going. Liza didn't mind this arrangement, and even put it about that he wasn't very fit, hinting at some past but serious illness he hadn't entirely got rid of or that might come back.

Liza would stand with folded arms by the kerb-edge outside the bookie's on many an afternoon because she had nothing better to do. She was a thin, thin-faced woman who must have been pretty, maybe even beautiful for eighteen months or so as a young girl, but who at thirty-odd had a tanned and raddled look sometimes seen in women who have spent half their lives in India. But Liza's big eyes and the light in them marked her as a working woman, and her perpetual thin-lipped wide-mouthed smile showed, as well as her inter-mittent intelligence, an acute sense of humour and wit. In face even of an uncomfortable situation, such as being asked to pay money when none was about, this wide smile would stay on her face, while she explained her predicament with a patience that only a smile would allow.

Outside the bookie's she would greet every man who went in and wish him luck and, weighing-up his face on exit, would either congratulate him or say: 'Better luck next time, duck.' When he was half-way across the street she would call, to his shock: 'It's allus the effing same, mate'—adding when he looked around: 'Ain't it?'

She got on well with the women in the street, often handed out kindling wood brought back from the tips. 'Tek this till your husband gets a job, duck.' Most mornings, having bundled the kids off to school at nine, she pushed her pram up the entry and set it in the middle of the street. Then she sat on it, balancing side-saddle, and pushed off with a sharp kick, the pram jerking slightly on its way over the cobbles and saving her a long walk to the street bottom.

People laughed: 'There goes old Liza again!' and she waved back in greeting. Some mornings she didn't feel so good: 'What the bleddy hell are yo' laughing at? You stand need to. Yo' ain't got two ha'pennies for a penny, either.' Or if anyone got in the way of her downward track: 'Clear out of the bleeding way, mental!'—as she rattled by on her pram of sackbags and rakes.

Her two kids, Alf and Harry, were in my class at school.

They were twins, Liza's first and last effort at having children. I became friendly with them, and we operated an alliance against any bully or gang that might set on us. Often, when none did, we mobbed each other, and in one scrabble by the school gates I made Harry's nose bleed like a tap. It was an accidental blow—or the weight of it was—and I felt so sorry for him that I gave up my black handkerchief to staunch the blood before sending him home. His mother had come back early that day from the tips because of the unmerciful rain, and on seeing blood all over his jumper she made him tell who had done it, or he would get two black eyes as well.

She waited for me by the bookies, and I walked all un-suspecting into a bust-up with Liza Atkin. 'I'll teach you to dirty our Harry's clothes like that,' she said, thumping away. 'You bleddy hooligan.' I tried thumping back, but I didn't get far, and not only did Harry's nose bleed that day, but mine bled as well, so I went into the house thinking aloud: 'Bleeding 'ell, what a life,' and had to make up a story of having skidded on a wet pavement and come a cropper on my snout, which for once mam believed saying I was daft enough for anything.

Liza was warned off the tips by the means-test man. Other scrapers put her wise by the newly laid road: 'Watch it, Liza. They're after us.' But she called: 'They wain't stop me doing what I like. If the getts want to tek my few bob off me I'll throw it in their effing phizzogs.'

The man followed her as if trailing a spy of some threatening nation, dogged her one Friday night from the steaming high banks of rammel to the scrapyard where her findings were weighed and paid for. She knew he was living in her shadow, and every hundred yards or so through the streets she would turn and wave her fist: 'You stand bleddy need! You stand need, you sponging blackgutted swine.'

'He was young enough to be my son,' she told my mother, unable to get the incident off her mind. Afterwards she stayed in the house for a week, sending the lads out now and again for a tin of milk or a loaf. My mother went to see if she was ill, but came back shaking her head and saying she wouldn't move from the new secondhand chair her husband hadn't long bought.

About this time Ted began going out every day—though not to a job. We only saw where he must have been (Liza, as my mother knew, wasn't the woman to give a straight answer) when the election came, because he walked down our street giving red flags and streamers to kids, and asking people to put red posters in their windows. He also came with a loudspeaker van handing out leaflets and newspapers. He smiled at everybody, but his eyes were like fires burning on ice.

Things began to improve, and when I asked why, somebody told me: 'Because there's going to be a war'—an ethical somersault at that time beyond my comprehension. But war came and, sure enough, everyone got work, though some were unlucky enough to be called up. One such must have been Robert the Welshman who was a gunner at an AA battery behind Serpent Wood. While the rest of his unit was doing PT one morning Robert slipped through the barbed wire and made his way into Nottingham. He was broke, cold, and fed-up to the teeth, and that night slept in an air-raid shelter, one of those brick and concrete erections set in the middle of the street.

Liza found him standing by the door at seven next morning. She was on her way to the shop for a packet of tea, and coming out spotted this forlorn short-arsed gunner blue with cold and ready to hand himself in at the nearest copshop for a cup of tea and slice of bread and marge—as he must earlier have handed himself into the army to get the same thing and then discovered he didn't like it.

Liza asked: 'Are you lost, duck?' and by the time she saw what it was all about, he was on her hands. He was a good-looking twenty-four, though his eyes shone from a sallow and troubled face.

'Yes, I am lost, missis. I don't know this town too well.'

'You'll soon pick it up,' she said. 'It gets a bit lively on Saturday night at the White Hoss. The ale's not bad there, but I don't drink much. It upsets my stomach.'

'I could do with a mug of tea, missis,' the soldier said. 'And a shave. I've been at war since this bloody war started, but I've had enough. My belly's full and overflowing with it, and I'm still hungry. I even signed on. Regular me! My mother wouldn't own me when I told her. Said she'd rather see me down the pit doing honest work.'

'Well,' Liza said, arms folded across her chest as if ready to hear a long story, 'you are kicking up a fuss. Not many blokes have been killed yet, have they?'

'But I'm not going to be there when it starts,' Robert said. 'All I want now is tuppence for a cup of tea. My throat's like dead cinders.'

'You wain't get far on tea,' she said, 'so come back with me and have a bit of breakfast. The old man wain't mind. He don't think much of this war, either, to tell you the honest truth.'

We soon heard that Liza had a lodger, and I saw him come out of her house that afternoon washed, shaved and spruced up in a borrowed suit on his way to the labour exchange to ask for a job. My mother discovered later that Liza had given him one of the lads' identity cards, and that Robert had rubbed the name out and changed it to his own, then marked the words RELEASED AS UNFIT FOR FURTHER SERVICE in his pay-book. The same evening he came back with employment cards and a job as a window cleaner.

Robert was popular in the street, and was referred to as 'Liza's deserter'. He was often seen on his way back from the library with an armful of books, and once he stopped me at the corner of the street, haunched to what he thought was my level but which left me looking down on him. 'Kid, come here.'

'What's up, mate?'

'Well,' he said, 'you look clever to me, man. Will you answer me a question. Just one question, not too hard for you.'

'Yes.'

'Well, do you know how Germany's going to lose the war?'

This stumped me. I wasn't sure that Germany was going to lose because I'd walked all around Nottingham looking at the defences of the town: some AA guns, one or two concrete barricades, tank traps, a few barracks and barbed-wire entanglements, a rusty Lewis Gun poking up into the low grey clouds above Trent Lane. 'Come on,' he said. 'You're slow. How is Germany going to lose the war?'

'I don't know.'

He put on a clever, know-all look, and stuck his face close to mine: 'Economic collapse,' he said. 'Economic collapse. Now go home and tell your dad. Go on, run.'

He settled down for a long stay in Nottingham, after his luck at meeting Liza and getting his papers so quickly in order. He wrote to a pal in Swansea, who sent his clothes and belongings. Robert earned fair money, pushing barrow and ladders from one set of offices to another, and even doing odd decorating jobs at week-end for the neighbours. One Sunday afternoon Liza was standing outside the bookies when a woman shouted: 'Liza, the redcaps are coming down street. Go and tell your Robert.'

One of the pair had a notebook, as if slowly checking door numbers, and while they were still far off Liza walked in to tell Robert to hide. She then came back to the bookies, calling as the redcaps drew near: 'Have you lost owt, mate?'

They didn't reply, and she said, while the other woman hissed at her from across the street for being so barmy: 'Maybe he's gone to France. You've come to the wrong place. Why don't you eff off to France and look for 'im there? Why don't you walk into one of them big German guns and search that?'

Her taunts were too much for one of them: 'That's where you ought to be, missis.'

She put her fist up: 'I'd like to see yo' try and send me there.'

'Leave her alone, Bill'—his mate pulled him away. To Liza's and everybody's surprise they didn't go for Robert, but carried on down the street to collar one of the Horley lads whom nobody knew had deserted. They found him sitting by the fire about to lift a mug of steaming tea to his lips, on the first day of his chosen freedom.

Robert went out window-cleaning one morning and didn't come back. A pair of redcaps waited at the bottom of his ladder and didn't even give him time to dry his hands. Liza swore blind to the police that she'd no idea her lodger was a deserter, and she couldn't think how he'd got hold of her lad's identity card and forged it. Robert had to serve three months in the glasshouse. He told the police he'd stolen the identity card from Liza's cupboard and altered it without her knowledge—otherwise Liza might have got three months as well.

She had a letter from Robert a year later saying he was out of the army and working on the Cardiff docks. She showed the letter to my mother who, knowing I was a good reader, passed it on to me. I could hardly believe my eyes when I saw that Robert had written: 'The war will be over soon because Germany is facing economic collapse. You see if I'm not right.'

I'll never forget the phrase, because a week later Germany invaded the USSR, and in his next letter Robert indicated that he had foreseen this because the Nazis needed Soviet Russia's raw materials to stave off economic collapse. My head spun at such political acumen, but in a way maybe he was right and there was nothing for the Germans to do but this, because they sure wouldn't have found any by invading England. Liza also got a letter from Robert's mother, thanking her for looking after her son while he was 'out with the army and caught by these troubles' as she put it.

Time was two-faced, and double-fisted: in one hand was what you expected, in the other what you didn't and nobody could ever say which was worse. We didn't know how he got into the Merchant Navy, but the next thing to happen Robert was killed on a convoy going to Archangel. I'd heard of this place from an old sweat next door who'd been there with the Marines after the First World War, and the only story he had to tell was of driving a horse and cart loaded with dead bodies back from the front. When I asked: 'Whose dead?' he answered: 'Whose do you think?' adding that it was the coldest place he'd ever been in. Such was the town that Robert never got to. Liza's face was scarred by the shock, which kept her morose for weeks. 'He was a nice chap,' she said. 'I feel as if I've lost a son of my own. I don't know, I don't.'

Her twin lads and husband Ted worked full blast on shell-cases at the factory, so nearly eight pounds a week came into the house. One day my mother was in when she lay their dinners out. 'If I gave that sort of stuff to your lot,' she reported, 'you'd give me the sack. It was cold, overcooked, and all one bleddy colour. Still, they love her for it, I will say that. And the house! Christ, it was so scruffy it wants stoving.' But neither sons nor husband complained, and in any case, I didn't think things were as bad as all that.

Liza still walked around in a faded blouse or jumper, and an old skirt. Her hair never seemed out of curlers, as if always keeping it ready to spring up wavy at the prospect of some fabulous wedding or mystery trip. She often pushed her old pram to the Park and brought washing home from American soldiers camped there. The copper chimney smoked over the backyards, and she pounded the dolly-ponch so strenuously into the zinc tub that it was a wonder the soldiers had anything to roister around the town in on most nights of the week.

She confided the difficulties of such a job over a cup of tea in our kitchen. 'The trouble is, all them Yanks look the same to me. When I go to the camp to tek their washing they all crowd round and I can't tell which is which, nor which ones gen me their washing. Anyway, it all gets snatched away and paid for, so I expect it's been all right up to now.'

My mother borrowed a pushcot and walked the couple of miles with her. They sometimes stopped for a drink at the Crown or Midland on the way back. 'We do have some bleddy fun, me and old Liza,' she said on one of those rare evenings when she could hardly cook the old man's tea.

One night, and next day, there were more machines droning through the overcast sky than in all the factories of Nottingham, and when Liza pushed her washing to the park that afternoon there was no one to claim or pay for it. The huts were deserted, the stunning noise of aeroplanes emphasizing locked and bolted doors. For the next few months Ted wore American shirts and underwear, since Liza's customers were never able to claim that particular consignment of spotless washing.

The war hadn't been over long before her own sons got called up. Time sped and telescoped, so that to Liza it seemed as if the war had never ended. There was still work, wasn't there?

I went on the booze with her two lads, Alf and Harry, before we were split three ways for the navy, the air force, and the infantry. We talked in a happy way about how our mothers had been friendly for the last ten years, how they had often gone on the Park together to collect washing from the Yanks. 'And it was the same pram old Liza pushed that she used to ride down street on to the tips before the war,' I laughed.

At this Alf stood up and threatened to bash my head in with a pint jar if I didn't stop saying such things about his mother. I was a bleddy liar, that's what I was. And an insulting bastard. I was on my feet, telling him to try it, if he dared, but Harry his brother pushed between us so that in a few minutes we shook hands, and ordered more pints. I'd never known they were so sensitive about Liza, though, funnily, it was the roughest of the pair who thought I wasn't respecting her. The other, Harry, was so dreamy I'd heard Liza shout down street to him on Friday night: 'Come on, get a move on you dozy bleeder. All the debt men are roaring for dough at the back door!'

Maybe that sort of thing had turned him dreamy and sensitive, though he was like that as a kid when they first came to live down our way. He was the one whose nose I'd fetched blood from years before, though he wasn't so dozy that he hadn't fetched a good drop from mine a time or two since. He'd turned out tall and a bit skinny, with awkward limbs and blue eyes that even factory work failed to make smart and quick. At his machine he was the sort that gashed his hand at least twice a week, or who every so often would be seen charging out of the factory for a bus to the Eye Infirmary, his hand over one eye. It was easier to picture him working at some haymaking job in the country instead of being stood before that fierce and neanderthal miller spitting suds and hot steel all over the place—in spite of the guards. Some women thought he lived almost without knowing he was born, saying that as a twin he must have had an easy time of it sliding out in the wake of Alf his first born brother.

Girls in the street swooned for him, swore they were out for a date not because he was so dopy (as rankled Alf and I teased) but because he never shouted when he talked, simply that.

'Maybe he's too idle to shout,' I said.

'Harry don't need to,' they jackalled back, from the lighted circle of a lamp-post. 'He'd just have to whisper, and we'd go running, wouldn't we, Lilly? So go on,' they said to us, 'run off. Collapse.'

It was an argument that couldn't go very far, for fear of saying too much against Harry, so we went catting away up the street, off to find more amenable fun in the pubs. The neighbourhood girls languished around their favourite lamp-posts like moths for all Harry wanted to do with them. He started courting, but with a quiet-looking girl with long hair called Jean who lived up Broxtowe, and he took her home to tea one Sunday.

Alf was there, and so was I, for it also turned into a final gathering before we parted for call-up. Liza cleaned the parlour and dusted the oddments of furniture, laid on a big tea of tinned fruit and cream, salmon and corned beef and beetroot. A new white blouse, and a brooch from Alf, set her off well among the rest of us. She made a fuss of Jean, went to the point of embarrassing Harry a time or two by hoping they'd be happy together.

'They deserve to, don't they, Ted?' she called to her husband, who hadn't yet moved from the fire. 'Young kids like these deserve a lot of happiness.' She dished out bigger

helpings than even they could manage: 'Come on, my angel,'
she said to Jean, 'get this chair drawn up and tuck in. You
never know how long this is going to last, eh? Come on,
duck. Ain't she handsome? They'll mek a smart pair, wain't
they, Ted?'

'Shurrup, mam,' Harry said. 'We ain't even engaged yet,
are we, love?'

'Not yet,' she came back, smiling. 'We're close to it if you
call me "love" in front of your mam, but it'll surprise me if
we ever are really engaged.' She wasn't so quiet as everybody
thought, and I knew already of a few rows and thump-ups
they'd had. It was no use telling Liza to tread it carefully, for
at a gathering like this she was in her element: 'That's what
they all say.'

Ted put down his paper. 'Liza, you silly old sod, shurrup.'

'Old? I'm not old yet. Don't tell me to shurrup, either. It
don't become you.'

'You're making 'em shy though,' Alf put in.

'Ah well,' she said. 'All right. I just want to see 'em happy.'

'We all do,' Ted jibed, with a wink at us. 'But don't cry
about it, will you?'

'Cry? Me cry? I got over that a long time ago, since I first
set eyes on yo', I should think. I wouldn't a done that either
if I hadn't broke that mirror and got fourteen years bad luck.
Look at 'em'—she turned to Jean and Harry—'They aren't
eating a bleddy thing.'

'Mam, stop swearing,' Harry said, thinking himself the only
one at the moment who could be firm with her and get away
with it.

'They're living off love. Who's bleddy-well swearing?
Don't talk to your mother like that, or you'll get my fist,
as big as you are. The way things are going there'll be a few
black eyes around here before we've done.'

'Who's cheeking you?' Harry said quickly. 'Nobody is.'

'Can I have some more bread and butter, Mrs. Atkin?'
Jean asked.

'You can have anything you like, my duck.' She almost

threw her arms around her. 'He ain't a bad lad, our Harry in't. You wain't go far wrong with him.'

Harry was secretive and unpredictable, and had been in the army a year before telling Liza he had fallen out with Jean. It was all off, he wrote to me in Malaya. I'm having too good a time these days to get married. She was too steady for me, and not my sort anyway. I suppose I'd be a lot better off if I knew what my sort bloody-well was, but I don't, and that's how it is. I'm fed'up to the eyeballs though. I don't know what I'm going to do when I get back home.

He agreed to stay another couple of years in the army because he couldn't think of anything better to do. I'd expected this, and when I wrote and mentioned a lot of other ways (among them emptying dustbins or sweeping roads) he didn't answer.

I'd already been back in Nottingham a while and having a good time when bad news spread grief like napalm over Liza's house. Ted left on the day of the telegram and wasn't seen for a week. Some thought him a coward and a rat, but both wanted to be alone with their wounds, out of sight of each other, and in the light that flickered through to her suffering Liza assumed he had gone back to his mother's, not blaming him for leaving her alone: due to such common injury they were in any case inseparable.

The message that Harry had been killed in Korea slammed into her face like an iron door that could never be opened again. It wasn't something she could avert, or appeal against, or even understand, but was felt to the core of her as being so final that she sat in the house for days, refusing all that helpful neighbours tried to feed her, shaking her head and not speaking. Harry's postcard photo had gone from the cheap stand-up frame on the dresser.

She walked up and down the street, as if nothing were the matter and she was merely on her way to and coming back from an errand. Arms folded, head down a little more than usual, she went up to the boulevard or on to Ilkeston Road, then came down the street as far as the factory on Faraday

Road, spending hours with no real purpose in her movement.

My mother would try talking to her. 'Come on, Liza, duck, let me get you some dinner. I've got a lovely piece of fish in the oven.' She took her arm, as if the touch of a hand would draw her along, but Liza said: 'Eff off,' with such stricken finality in her eyes that they had to let her go. One woman thought they should tell a doctor and get her to hospital or home, but Ted returned and said: 'She'll be all right in a day or two.'

She came down the street with a loaf in her hand and, in spite of the tears streaming down her face, bit a piece off the bread now and again. Ted looked after her, but it was a long time before she could speak about Harry, and even then couldn't remember as many things about him as she would have liked. Ted wouldn't say: 'Do you remember when he did this or said that' for fear of throwing her—and himself—back on the first spikes of anguish. They received a letter from one of his friends in hospital telling how their company had been attacked by American planes spreading napalm bombs intended for the communist lines close by. Dozens of other blokes had copped it in that little balls-up and, Harry's friend added, I'm lucky to be alive myself.

Liza was walking along a lane near Wollaton, and remembered how, at the beginning of the war, Harry and Alf had been evacuated to Worksop. Harry had been sick all the way there on the bus, and she laughed now to think of it.

She fetched them back a few months later when no bombs looked like falling, and one day Harry came home from school with a belt of live machine-gun bullets over his shoulder. It was his loving possession, and I remember him saying that maybe it would come in handy in case the Germans ever landed. Reassembling the ferocious looking bandolier one dinner-time, a couple slid from the hob into the fire. Dreamy intent Harry leapt into life shouting: 'Scatter! There's a shell in the grate'—and the room emptied but for Ted, who poked the bullets out before they'd time to explode. Liza went to the school and asked the teacher to take them away in case danger was done.

When Ted was on nights Harry slept on the sofa downstairs, in order to get her and Alf up when the sirens went: 'Come on, the guns is going'—though neither took notice but stayed fast asleep, so that he eventually got into bed with Alf and dozed the air raid off beside him.

Right from fourteen he was a bogger with the girls, she smiled, because he was the quiet and good-looking sort. Many's the time he came home with lipstick smeared over his shirt, and once when Liza said: 'What's that red stuff on your collar?' trying to shame him, he answered, as bold as brass:

'Are you blind, mam? It's lipstick.'

Or: 'It's bugs blood.' Neither of the lads would come in earlier than two on Saturday night, so Liza would leave the key in the scullery window. One evening he stumbled on his way upstairs and woke her, though the old man stayed fast asleep. 'Is that you, Harry?'

He went into the room and switched the light on: 'Hello, ma.'

'Did you have a good time?'

This made him laugh. 'Smashing. I'm dead beat, though.'

'I'll get you a big breakfast in the morning. Eggs, bacon and tomatoes. What's her name, then?'

'Jean, if you want to know.'

'Course I want to know. Have you bin boozing?'

'The usual'—meaning a good bit.

'You ought to bring her home to tea,' she said. 'Sunday tea' —never thinking he'd be bothered. He bent down and kissed her, then clicked off the light and went to bed.

The lane narrowed, took her through a field, over a stile and up a low hill, woods to the right and distant council houses to the far left. Clouds were low and grey like battle-ships, and the warmth hustled them along, making the grass move as well and smell fresh and hot like new bread.

There seemed no end to the things she could remember about him. A flicker of lightning festered over the black sky of Nottingham. Storms made her afraid, and she walked more quickly towards bus noises on the main road. I don't know who to blame, she thought, but go on, rip and claw the effing world to pieces. Tear up that bleddy town, sling it to hell.

On the bridge a railwayman said to her: 'What's up, duck? What are you crying for?'—but she walked on. Cold rain woke her, and the storm burst, shattering the trees.

A bus took her to Radford, and children were coming out of school, running to dodge what was left of the downpour. Liza walked up the yard towards her back door. The kitchen window had been smashed weeks ago when some kid threw a pebble, and the space it made was shaped like a black butterfly.

She put the light on, which brightened the kitchen, then set the kettle to boil. Korea was a world, a word, as far off now as somebody else's dream, that had killed Harry, called him up and bombed him to ashes for no good reason, like when you have too many kittens you dunk some in a copper. It wasn't necessary, it was wrong, the bad thing to do. She remembered the black agonizing haze of Alf's birth, then Harry came after, a dream child who always wanted to stop playing shadow to his tougher hard-fighting brother. And now Alf hadn't got his would-be shadow any more which, funnily enough, took away much of his brawling, quietened him down as if dead Harry had left more in his brother than at first met the eye. Ah well. She couldn't cry any more. But he'd been killed for nothing, for some foul thing, she thought—as Ted had tried to tell her time and time again, but she was too struck down to understand. There was nothing on the face of the earth that would have made her say: 'It was worth it. That's a good thing to die for.' The kettle boiled and she reached up to switch on the light, realizing, before her fingers touched the switch, that it had been on for some time.

I left Nottingham and set off on my travels, still lured by islands and oceans, panoramic fields fanning out to green woods on the horizon, as I had been that day at ten when I'd wanted to leave but had been pulled back by Alf—who didn't get the same kick out of unattainable goals as I did. Though I was away my mother in her letters never failed to tell anecdotes about Liza, and keep me informed on what was happening to her.

Liza went to one of the big local factories and asked for a job. She did sweeping up at first, then progressed to sit-down work as a viewer, checking steel elbows with a depth gauge to make sure each piece was within specifications. It was a mechanical job, and would have been monotonous during the years she stayed at it, but to Liza it implied so much trust in her that she enjoyed every one of the thousands passed each day. The first morning in the shop a steward said:

'I'll put your name down for the union.'

'What union?' she demanded, leaning on her sweeping brush. 'Don't be too hasty with me, you fawce bogger.'

He was a lame man, and hobbled a yard off at this. 'It's the Amalgamated Engineering.'

'All right then,' she said, 'put me down for it. But next time have less of your lip. How much do I owe you?'

A dozen women were on viewing, and Liza sat with them along a bench. She was a thin-faced forty-five now, looked small and angular compared to some of her more buxom mates, as if she lived on fresh air, they said. And she still wore an old skirt and cardigan, and button-up shoes cut at the sides to make way for her bunions. 'What do you spend your money on, Liza?' one of the women called.

'Mind your own business. I spend it on fruit machines at the club. Tanner a time. Used to be a penny, but they aren't satisfied with that any more. Everything's going up and up. So there I stand, Friday, Sat'day and Sunday nights pulling that handle and waiting to win a fortune.'

'It'd be cheaper to watch television, Liza.'

'It'd be cheaper to do something else as well. There's nowt but adverts on telly though, and they hurt my eyes. Still, it tells you what's best to buy, and that's good of 'em, but that flickering gets on my nerves. Anyway, I used to think stuff advertised on telly was good but now I don't. If owt's adver-tised on telly I don't buy it. But even that ain't much good either, because nearly everything's advertised, so as far as I can see you might as well tek a running jump at yourself, except that nowt's ever been any good, so you just have to buy what you can and hope for the best. Most of what you get for your money you might as well sling on the fire-back, that's what I think, and if we didn't have any of this rammel we wouldn't be any worse off. So spending it on fruit machines ain't all that much of a waste.'

'Don't you ever win owt at all, though?'

'Sometimes, duck. But I'm a bleddy fool. It all goes back. Ted said he'd black my eye if I didn't keep off them machines. Mind you, I spend a few bob on our Alf's kids. He's got two now, you know. They're only babies still, but I can't see 'em without whatever they want.'

'It looks as if he's making up for the lad you lost, Liza.'

'He'd better. But maybe he is. Have you got a fag, duck?'

'That's about the fiftieth. Here y'are, though.'

'Never mind,' Liza said. 'When we go on strike I'll get a job and pay you back.' Liza was a wag, life's fag-lighter, wick flint and fuel working in unison, a combustuous spark tindering the whole line of women into laughs all day long. 'Here she comes,' the shop steward said one morning: 'The apostle of industrial unrest.'

'You speak when you're spoken to,' she threw at him, hanging up her coat so that the sandwich packet jutted squarely from it. 'I don't get much rest at this rotten place.'

'You will,' he answered. 'We'll be on short time soon.'

'Then get on with it, or we'll put somebody else in your job. I want some rebate on that union money.'

'Go on, Liza. You'll only spend it on the machines.'

'No, I'm stopping that. You cheeky bastard. Shuffle off to the Cripples' Guild and get that gammy leg seen to.'

'Oh Liza, you are awful,' one of the women said, trying not to laugh.

'Go on, he knows I don't mean it, don't you Albert, my old flower?' White with rage, he was ready to walk off, hardly smiled when she left her stool and gave him a kiss.

'You're a sod,' he said. 'I don't know what we're going to do with you.'

'Pension me off,' she suggested.

'You're too young. You don't look a day over sixty-five.' She was suddenly on the bench doing a skirts-up can-can to the grinding roar of machinery, her singing mouth an apparition of silence among total noise. She got down to clapping from the rest: 'I'm not a day over twenty, more like it.'

When the foreman came along he would whistle loudly so that work could be resumed before he showed his face. One day he didn't give his customary warning and two women were sacked. 'What does he expect?' Liza said, 'work ourselves dry so's we can get laid off or get put on short time?'

They went on four days a week, then three days, and wage-packets dropped because, so the shop steward explained, work was being diverted to the Coventry branch, where people were already on a full week and being asked to do more and more overtime.

The whole department went to the canteen for a meeting. On the far platform of the tobacco-smoke and sunfilled hall a speaker was suggesting they walk out straightaway and hold a rally in Slab Square, where they could really air their views. Then a more moderate orator put a resolution that they ask the management to reconsider the system whereby Coventry had so much work and Nottingham less than necessary for the men to live on. At which they could return to work and wait patiently for an answer.

The girdered and pillared hall was half filled, but men and women were coming in all the time, doors crashing for each new group so that no space remained by the end of the meeting. It was eleven-thirty, and from beyond the serving hatches came smells of cabbage and gravy and custard for thousands of midday dinners. Liza listened to each speech, taking in every word of their plain arguments. She edged her way nearer the stage, forcing bony shoulders between the insensitive slab-backs of two men, until one gave way and let her through to another contest.

Shouts from the back of the hall increased, gathered into a wave that swept against the platform. The more violent wanted action now, instead of putting it off for a week or a fortnight—'for as long as the management can stall and delay,' one cried.

'A walkout is inevitable, so let's go.' Liza's head turned, to see this speaker pulled on the stage by his mates: a tall young man of twenty-odd, just in from the Turnery where, he said, they were all for a strike, and no messing.

'I'm willing to go out, even though I've got a wife and kids like the rest of you.' He spoke about the bosses and the management, saying there'd never be any peace until they were got rid of, because they didn't know how to run the place. It should be handed over to those who did. A demonstration was called for by a vast field of hands: on Friday morning they would march downtown to Slab Square.

The words and phrases, dull and empty perhaps to those who haven't worked in a factory, or owned one, thrilled Liza with their lucidity and common sense. At the same time she felt a sort of unspecified fear at the young man's words, though once she got used to the tone of them he reminded her of Harry sprung back to life and saying decisively all the things he should have wanted to say because of his useless death, only now his face was harder for having been through the fire of it, and his words were sharp and loud because all uncertainty had been carried away by the possibility of some kind of action. 'What are you crying for, missis?' a man said, not so moved by the young man's speech as Liza.

'I'm not crying for yo',' she said, pushing to get nearer the platform. 'I had a son like him, so keep your trap shut.'

'If we go out now we can win, but we'll get nowt by staying quiet like good little boys. What are you waiting for? Are you frightened they'll come and tek your TV sets back next week? Well, you could have plenty to see without looking at them. And anyway that'd put a few television blokes out of work as well, which is just what we want, because the more out the better. If the HP firms want to fetch your car or motorbike back they wain't have enough bailiffs to go round—not to mention enough warehouses to put them in if they have! Anyway, you've all got two feet to walk or run on. I'm not being funny either. And don't think you'll be fed-up at being off wok because you can allus find plenty to do while you're out on strike. I suppose,' he went on, 'you think the landlords will be after you if you can't pay your rent? Maybe. But don't forget there are ten thousand of us at this factory, and if they want our families as well on the street, let's see 'em put us there. Not that you'll go short of snap, because I know where there's loads on it, and clothes, and everything we need! But seriously . . .'

Liza laughed with the rest, a ferocious nudge at the man next to her. 'We wanted a few blokes like him before the war.'

'Ay,' the man said, 'the balloon'll go up one day, especially with young boggers like him up there.'

'Who is he then?' Liza asked.

'Don't ask me. But he's got the gift of the gab all right.' She stayed quiet in the forest of legs and arms and shoulders, ignoring their blind pressure as long as she was able to hear:

'When I was in the army I had to get vaccinated for *small*pox. They tried it the first time, but nothing happened. It wouldn't take. Then a second jab and it still wouldn't take. So they tried again—five bloody times altogether, until they gave it up as a bad job. My arm looked like the top of a pepperpot, and felt just as hot.'

'Well, they can give us what we want in this dispute (and they will, make no mistake about it) and they can give us a raise when we force the boggers to it, but as far as I'm concerned, it'll be like them smallpox jabs I had. It wain't take. It's not a raise here and a bit of an improvement there that we want—none of it'll take. It's a whole bloody change'—his wide-apart fists gave a slow forceful turning motion as if at the wheel of some great ship and making a violent alteration in its course—'a turnover from top to bottom. . . .'

Liza found herself trapped. Her feet edged forward, but even the use of sharp elbows couldn't free her from the sea-like movement towards the row of swing doors. She was urged down the steps, kept upright by the rapid working of her feet, and out into the road. It was blocked by people leaving the factory, many running from departments that had sent no representatives to the meeting.

She walked up the street at just gone twelve, awed by the unfamiliar gap presented by the rest of the day, too stunned for a moment to wonder how it could be crossed. Women stood at yardends to watch this unexpected purposeful walk-out from the vast factory whose machines appeared to be breathing their last before a host of other machines began to demolish the lot.

'What's going off?' they cried. 'What's up?'

'We're on strike,' Liza called.

'What for?'

'We've had enough, that's why.'

There was little talking, only the walk and roll of in-numerable sud-deadened boots sounding on the pavement. The pour-out was so great and quick that people walked up the middle of the street, and a bread van making its way against them did so without once splitting the air with its hooter— as it would if children played in its track on other days.

'What's happening?'

'We've had enough,' Liza called. 'We're packing in, duck. It's as much as anybody can effing-well stand.' She walked more slowly, feeling tireder than if she had in fact done the stint of a full hard day. Only some youths from the Frame Shop brawled their way through, discussing what was on at the pictures that afternoon.

By the backdoor she noted the old pram that had carried so much: children, household belongings on their various flits, then valuable scrap from the tips, and washing for the Americans. It was on its last legs now, she thought, rolling back the cover to look, though it was still useful for fetching coke from the gasworks in snowtime, or shoving the family wash to the new laundrette on Saturday morning. Still, if the dole times came back—they only seemed like yesterday when she dwelt on them—the old man might have to put on sound front wheels and get it going again.

Gas bumped into flame under the kettle, and she took two slices of collared-head and a tomato from the larder and sat down to a midday dinner. The wall needed papering, was losing its fresh smartness of navy-blue with pin stripes. They used to joke about how it looked like Alf's demob shirt and suit, saying that when he put them on and stood against the wall you wouldn't know he was in the room. Maybe I can do it while we're on strike, she thought, recalling how the young man speaking in the canteen had said nobody ought to be idle at such a time.

She heard rain teeming down, but rather hoped for something wrong with her ears than that it was going to be a wet day, since she'd arranged to link up with her pals at the Slab Square meeting.

The old man stopped snoring, kissed her and got out of bed. He dressed rapidly and clattered downstairs to get some breakfast. This was the best time of the day, when Ted had gone and she dozed in his even warmer patch for an hour. Often she wished all these early mornings could be joined into one uniform life of ease and freedom, but suddenly her eyes opened and, without having made a decision, she stood on the cold lino fastening her skirt and pulling a jumper over her vest. Rain threw itself across the backyards.

Bacon and egg spat fat across the frying-pan, and the sandwich she made was jammed in the pocket of her plastic mac. A pair of galoshes looked after her feet, and with the mac hood up she stood in the doorway, her body unwilling to commit itself into such a fanatical downpour of grey rain. Its cold wall wafted against her face, the heavy smell of it hypnotizing her as it jerked out of the drainpipe like a phosphorescent hand splaying over the yard. Had the factory been working she wouldn't have heard it: rain fell as if to bruise the houses and enter through the slates. She was reminded of a few days at the seaside thirty years ago, when the noise of waves humping the promenade had been gradually lessened by someone shutting the boarding-house windows one by one, cutting the sound but for a low distant hiss. The rain drew off in this way and she walked into what remained.

She felt good, being on strike; it was a way of doing damage to those who bossed the world about. She was amazed that news of it was in all the papers, according to which the gaffers in their big cars weren't at all liking what they called loss of production, but which Liza saw as their loss of profits. Neither did the government like the strike, which surprised her even more—to think that their plain factory could make a government feel that way. She was almost afraid that coppers would be set on them to try and stop it.

Hundreds of men and youths stood hemmed into the pavement by mounted police. Liza got off a trolley bus, pointed at the police and called in her sharpest tone: 'Are they coming down with us as well? Christ, even the coppers have got a grievance! Hey, why don't you tek your horse out of the wet?'

A faint smile came on the copper's face.

'Where's all your pals, Liza?' a man shouted.

'You're asking me.' She looked along the lines and the only explanation seemed that they were still toasting their toes by the fire. All were men, dressed in trilby and mac, cap and overcoat, many smoking patiently, as if waiting outside the biggest pub in the world for opening time, Liza thought, but changing her mind about this at banners appearing with rhymes and slogans written over them, and at the grim expression on men's faces holding them high. Some youths wore ban-the-bomb badges, talked and laughed in a group, as if this wouldn't be the last industrial argument they'd take part in.

A rough column formed in the road, and Liza went towards the head of it. She felt it strange to see such a host of workers away from the factory, out on a main road and not divided by departments or hindered from shaking each other's hand by machines and benches. But in spite of the odd voice lifted now and again she was also surprised at how quiet so many men could be. She doubted whether anyone would realise a demonstration was so close if they'd been walking only a street away, or were yet to come from around one of the nearby corners. Why aren't they all shouting? she wondered. They should be bawling themselves dry.

She placed herself near Albert the shop steward, who welcomed her: 'I'll bet you've never been out with two thousand men in your life before, Liza!'

The column made a question mark around the traffic

island, and a bus driver wished them luck as he went by, to which Liza retorted: 'That's all very well, but you should be down here with us, mate.'

'One day, missis, I will.'

'You'll be laughing on the other side of your face by then, though.'

'Leave him be, Liza,' Albert said. 'You've got too much on it.' They descended into town towards Slab Square, passing rows of heavily laden shops fronting the rain. Liza offered her bacon-and-egg sandwich: 'No thanks, duck. I had my breakfast.'

'I didn't'—biting a bay into its rugged coast. 'I can never eat a thing till after ten. I just had a cup o' tea. P'raps we'd better get used to starving a bit now, though.' She lifted her hand to sling the rest of the sandwich away, but Albert stopped her. 'Don't do that. Get it down you.'

The column was like a magnet, pulling in stragglers and late arrivals. Liza shivered in the rain at one of many traffic stops, though her face felt like a stoked-up fire. There was a shaking of rain off macs, a stamping of feet. 'What are you on strike for?' a woman laden with shopping called from the kerb.

'Because we've had enough,' Liza told her. 'There's too much short time in our bleddy factory, and we're going to put a stop to it. Wouldn't you though, eh?'

'You all ought to be shot,' a man shouted. He had a freckled pug-face and a tonsure of ginger hair. Though dressed with great care his appearance was shabby, as if he'd been all night in the street.

'Why aren't yo' at wok, then?' the shop steward bawled. Liza was surprised, disturbed to see that not everyone was on their side. He didn't look up to much either. 'You and your lot want to try shooting us,' she cried.

'You want the dole back,' he retorted bravely.

A youth stepped out for him: 'Looking for a punch-up, scab?'—but was dragged back by two older men: 'Leave him be. He'll get it when the time comes.'

'You're a dirty Red,' he snarled, now at a safe distance, a pillar-box his only ally.

'You'll be red if I smash my fist in your clock'—this from the man whose loud voice Liza had heard in the canteen. In the Square, he was first on the platform giving a logical though somewhat wild speech. A heckler called that instead of being so hot-headed he'd do better to get the dispute made official, then at least there'd be strike pay. Liza stood on one of the wide slab parapets to see and hear better, noticing many umbrellas now opened among the crowd.

'Don't worry about strike pay,' the young man called, bare-headed and wearing a long plain mackintosh. 'If everybody was on strike there'd be no call for money or pay for a good while. As for all this stuff about official and unofficial strikes, that's the Tory press and the Tory union bosses trying to kid you. There ain't no difference between an official and un-official strike because a strike's a strike, it don't matter what name you give it. The unions and the bosses say: "Go back to work, lads, then we can mek the strike official." ' Laughter. 'They're hand in hand with each other, like sweethearts who can't make up their minds whether or not to get married—though they'll do us a lot of damage before they finally break it off, if we let 'em. Nowadays you've got to fight the unions before you can fight the bosses, and you can't win a thing until you've shown both of them that you mean business.'

Liza cheered the pro-strikers, feeling, now that the defences of her galoshes had been penetrated, as if she were standing in three feet of water. The speeches didn't get down to warming her, but such discomfort was only half noticed when so many others had to put up with it as well. Some speculated on the far-off presence of cameras in windows above department stores; a man near Liza suggested they might belong to the police who were getting photos of the speakers; others wondered whether they weren't TV cameras collecting to-night's news; Liza shouted out something to the effect that maybe both TV and police might even collaborate on an occasion like this.

'I knew we'd get what we wanted,' Liza said, exulting before those along the bench at how she had marched in the demonstration. Yet when her work became heavy and slow, about four-thirty in the afternoon, she remembered her feelings at the time of the strike, and felt let down, not by the people walking with her, but by something lacking in the atmosphere. It wasn't total or decisive enough, though no one person (or even mob) could have made it so, and what gnawed at her was the possibility that she might not be alive when some mysterious spark touched off the explosion that she felt inside her. She thought that such a downing of tools as had taken place meant little because instead of coming back to work they should have stayed out solid and gone on from there. It was as if she had been tricked, or had tricked herself by expecting too much after that first meeting in the canteen. Something other than the mere petty end of an industrial dispute was sensed by her, the half felt presence of an abyss that she would willingly cross even if its hardships were worse than any she had yet known. When one of the women said how good it was that if the workers came out solid they could win, win, win, Liza shouted back at her and the others on the bench for being loons who'd let anybody do them down. 'You ain't won because you was too frightened to stay out and win it proper.' They were uneasy, thought she was losing her old sense of humour, but as the memory of the strike grew less intense Liza seemed to become herself again.

'It's funny, ain't it?' she called one day.

'What's funny, Liza?'

'That everybody's got different colour eyes. You'd think they'd all be the same. It's never struck me before.' There was laughter, followed by agreement. It was true now that Liza mentioned it. Why did everybody have different colour eyes? They ought to be the same, really. 'They say we started off as monkeys,' Liza said. 'I read it somewhere.'

'Some of us still are!'

'Maybe we'll end up having the same colour eyes. You never know, do you? There'd be no difference then between anybody. It's funny when you think of it like that. I wouldn't mind though, would you, duck?'

*

Which winds me back to this London cop-station—having taken over twenty years and a great circle of half the world to get here since first glimpsing the land beyond Nottingham when I was going to run away from home with Liza's son. It's four o'clock in the morning and the others are asleep, galley-slaves to an idea folded over the oars of their detained bodies that continually move because they can't find an easy position. It's twelve hours since I had a drink, but thinking about Liza walking in the rain has slaked my thirst a while longer.

Early in November following the strike I saw a pack of kids in Radford pushing a load of combustible rubbish down the street, balancing it high on a vehicle I recognized as Liza's old pram.

'What are you going to do with that?'

'Burn it, mester, on Bonfire Night,' the ringleader told me.

'The pram, I mean.'

'Yeah. Liza gen it to us. It ain't no good. We'll chuck it on top.'

'It's too good to burn,' I said.

He pushed the rubbish aside for a skilful reappraisal of the wheels. 'P'raps we'll use it then.'

I was in Nottingham more often, and on one occasion I heard that Liza Atkin had died. I couldn't believe it for a while. 'She wasn't old'—as if that would make it a lie and bring her back, pram and all.

'She was fifty-five though,' my mother said.

'So are you,' I reminded her, in case she thought it a ripe old age. 'What did she die of?'

I was never told, only that 'she had suffered, poor woman,' my mother said, 'because I was with her and know.' She went on to say that Liza as a young woman had been beautiful, and a smart dresser. This was the first time I'd heard anyone claim to have known Liza before she pushed her pram down our street that windy day before the war, and I didn't know whether my mother was making it up, or if she really had discovered a lost friend of her youth in some conversation I hadn't overheard or heard about.

Again she said: 'Liza was ever so smart as a young woman,' and though I could accept the word beautiful (her hair stayed black right up to her death) the adjective 'smart' seemed impossible to fit on her. Yet my mother was convinced, and in a strange way, hearing this word 'smart' used about Liza as a young woman made her death seem an even deeper blow than if I hadn't heard the word.

Several other people died that year. Liza wouldn't stand with folded arms outside the bookie's any more, but I imagined her dead, saying as the others came in: 'Any luck, mate?'—as she had on innumerable times by the bookie's in the street. Then, when some new arrival was half-way across to the gates of hell: 'It's allus the effing same, ain't it?' The stunned shock at hearing this would help him over the heart-breaking part of his transition before final blackness.

In spite of the heavy air in the cell I take out a cigar I've been saving all through the pushing and cordon-breaking and shouting and dragging. I light up. Liza was a good woman who lived a life worth thinking about on a long night like this. If anybody ever asks me why I got hauled in by the coppers maybe I'll tell them about her.

One day, for a glimpse of old trees and views, (or sentinel coppices smudged beside tall chimneys of derelict limekilns), I took a bus to Trowel and walked back over Balloon House hill. Patches of white frost illumined fields on either side of the straight road. Weak but welcome sunshine penetrated the mists of Trowel Moor and Hemlock Stone. It was a good day in spite of winter.

I met Alf near Wollaton Village. His two boys, of five and seven, honed along the road with their new shoes as we made for the Admiral Rodney pub. Alf had a house on a nearby estate. It was bitterly cold, but we stayed at a backyard where no one else sat, coaxing the level of our pint jars lower and lower. As always, talk was about the past, and of how life had slowed down now—though not so much as a day like this indicated.

The subject suddenly changed: 'My two young 'uns broke their heart when mam died,' Alf said, his grey eyes looking vacant, dealing as they were with something profound and sad, 'as young as they are. She spent so much on 'em I used to get mad at times. They wain't forget mam in a hurry.' The kids played while we drank our beer. One was the spitten-image of Alf, but the other resembled Liza in his hard, all-enduring, well-shaped face. He was the youngest, but his brother seemed afraid of his ferocious way of fighting. Perhaps Alf remembered our last meeting in a pub, when we'd nearly come to blows over Liza:

'Mam was rough. In fact they didn't make 'em any rougher than mam. You remember that strike at the factory? I don't think she knew what it was all about, but she knew whose side she was on. I think she enjoyed it as well. The only complaint she'd got was that it worn't rough enough for her. She wanted a real blow-up. Mam was a good woman, I'll say that.' He looked at his two kids fighting by the garage door: 'Stop that, you little bleeders, or you'll get a pasting. Come on'—he turned to me—'you don't knock 'em back like you used to. I'll get a couple more.'

'Thanks,' I said, sliding the mug over. 'Let's drink to Liza. She was one of the best.'

'You can say that again'—keeping a good eye still on his kids. Then he hooked up the mugs and made for the pub's back door.